No Man's Land

VE Sept 18

No Man's Land

Graham Greene

Edited by James Sexton

ET REMOTISSIMA PROPE

Modern Voices

Modern Voices
Published by Hesperus Press Limited
4 Rickett Street, London sw6 1ru
www.hesperuspress.com

No Man's Land and *The Stranger's Hand* first published in *Mornings in the Dark: the Graham Greene Film Reader* in 1993
First published by Hesperus Press Limited, 2005
No Man's Land © Verdant S.A., 1993
The Stranger's Hand © Verdant S.A., 1993

Foreword © David Lodge, 2005
Introduction © James Sexton, 2005

Designed and typeset by Fraser Muggeridge studio
Printed in Jordan by Jordan National Press

ISBN: 1-84391-109-4

Contents

Foreword

Graham Greene belonged to the first generation of British writers who grew up with the movies, and his work, like that of his contemporaries Evelyn Waugh, Henry Green and Christopher Isherwood, was deeply influenced by the new medium. What Greene learnt from cinema was how to hold his readers in the coils of a suspenseful plot while exploring unsettling moral and metaphysical themes, and how to evoke character and milieu with the verbal equivalent of cinematic close-ups and pans. His literary imagination, however, did not easily translate in the opposite direction. Nearly every novel he wrote was eventually made into a film, but very few have been good films, and only one is a classic: *The Third Man*, directed by Carol Reed, which Greene scripted himself (with a little help from Orson Welles, who provided the famous line about Switzerland's contribution to civilisation being the cuckoo clock).

It was the success of *The Third Man* which prompted Greene to propose soon afterwards another film that would have been very similar in style and substance. *No Man's Land* is the 'treatment' Greene wrote for that film, which was never made. Like *The Third Man*, it is a mystery thriller set in occupied Europe a few years after the end of the Second World War and early in the Cold War. Like *The Third Man*, it involves the quest of one male character for another to whom he is emotionally attached, in circumstances of extreme jeopardy, with the additional spice of female love interest. In both stories the personal and the political are entwined thematically as well as in the narrative. What is distinctive about *No Man's Land* is the religious and specifically Catholic strand in the story, including the use of a slightly dubious Marian shrine as the setting for two of its most dramatic scenes.

A film treatment is usually a detailed summary of what the proposed film would actually show. Greene's treatments are formally indistinguishable from his short stories, and the two paired together in this book include many touches that would be impossible to replicate in the film medium. For example:

> ...before Brown had reached the door Starhov was already asleep – like the dead, like the effigy on his own tomb, Brown thought, except that there would be no effigy on the tomb of one who had committed the crime of trust.

Conceivably, a carefully composed shot of the sleeping Starhov could evoke the effigy simile, but there is no way that Brown's paradoxical and very Greeneian thought could be conveyed visually. Greene made explicit in his treatments things that would become part of the subtext of the projected films, or disappear altogether.

'Trust' is a keyword – *the* keyword – of *No Man's Land*. The Cold War is the political expression of profound mutual mistrust between the Soviet bloc and the Western Powers, and has given rise to an elaborate system of espionage, the world of the double agent and the double-cross which always fascinated Greene from adolescence onwards. Starhov's 'crime' in trusting Brown's word is political, just as Brown's duty to betray him is political. The political is opposed to the moral. 'If we loved God do you think all this would exist?' Clara asks Brown, meaning by 'all this' the violence and treachery and futile conspiracies of the Cold War. Brown answers that he can't get further than loving a woman; but in order to do that you have to trust, in spite of the risk of betrayal. A final twist in the narrative hints that Clara, the German Catholic with whom Brown falls instantly and irrevocably in love (as she with him), is eventually unfaithful to him.

This relationship sometimes seems sketched rather than fully realised, but it might have been more convincing when acted out on screen. Also it is relevant that religious belief and sexual promiscuity were improbably combined in Greene's real-life mistress at this time, Catherine Walston, with whom he fell in love at their first meeting. James Sexton, the editor of this volume, is absolutely right to see *No Man's Land* as driven by the novelist's jealous and obsessive passion for Catherine, who was later to serve as the model for another, more complex and believable heroine, the Sarah of *The End of the Affair*. The hero's name seems to be a teasing reference to the author's.

If the scenes between Brown and Clara sometimes come dangerously close to self-parody, the second tale in this volume actually began as a conscious exercise in self-parody; but in many ways it is a more controlled piece of writing than *No Man's Land*, and it is a pity that it is unfinished. The first two paragraphs of *The Stranger's Hand* were submitted by Greene under the name of N. Wilkinson for a *New Statesman* competition, set by Walter Allen in May 1949, to write the best imitation or parody of the opening lines of a novel by any writer called Green or Greene. His entry was awarded the second prize. His friend, the Italian film director Mario Soldati, persuaded him to continue the story in earnest as a film treatment, but Greene apparently lost interest in the project, and another hand eventually brought it to a conclusion so that the movie could be made. But the sizeable fragment of the original treatment is first class.

Greene, who wrote memorably about his own alienated childhood, was always skilful at creating unhappy, sensitive children, and the plight of the eight-year-old Roger Court, posted like a parcel to a strange foreign city, Venice, to meet a long-absent father who fails to turn up, is vividly and movingly portrayed. The rituals with which the boy seeks to distract himself, like the improvised game of cricket, and the moments when his courage and self-control suddenly give way to helpless tears, are beautifully judged. Here, as in his story 'The Basement Room', which he adapted very successfully for the cinema as *The Fallen Idol*, Greene perhaps took a leaf out of Henry James's book, specifically from *What Maisie Knew*, in rendering a naive point of view in a well-formed and eloquent style, so that we apprehend both the child's innocence and the seriousness of what is at stake in the adult world.

There are several similarities between this tale and *No Man's Land*. Again the background is Cold War espionage and intrigue; again confrontation across the frontiers of disputed territory serves as a metaphor for moral and emotional disconnection:

> ...he turned on the bedside light to read his letter... 'Dear Roger' (the phrase had the same distance as 'my father': they seemed to be signalling to each other tentatively over the No Man's Land of two years, a waste filled with the wreckage of other lives than their own).

Just as Greene's jealously possessive feelings about Catherine Walston provided much of the emotional fuel for *No Man's Land*, so (one might speculate) did his guilt about deserting his own children, when he separated from his wife Vivien, find expression in the compassionate portrait of Roger, and in Major Court's stoical sense of having failed as both parent and policeman. The way Roger uses the juvenile adventure stories he reads as a way of interpreting his own experiences parallels the intertextual allusions to Turgenev in *No Man's Land*. Both treatments exhibit Greene's incomparable ability to evoke the sense of place, whether it is the relatively unfamiliar Harz Mountains, or the hackneyed setting of Venice, which he makes us see afresh.

Hesperus has performed a valuable service in making widely available for the first time a reliable edition of these two little-known texts, written between *The Heart of the Matter* and *The End of the Affair*, when Greene was at the height of his powers as a novelist. They are minor works, but Graham Greene is one of the select group of modern writers of whom it can be said that almost nothing they wrote is without interest or evidence of a unique literary gift.

– *David Lodge, 2005*

Introduction

Despite the fact that Graham Greene's 15,000-word film treatment *No Man's Land* is briefly mentioned in the standard Graham Greene bibliography published in 1979, none of Greene's many biographers discuss it, or even appear to know of its existence. To date, the only critical reference to Greene's Cold-War thriller is a brief discussion published in Judith Adamson's 1984 book, *Graham Greene and Cinema*. Since its purchase from a New York book dealer in 1966, the typescript has been stored in the Graham Greene collection at the Harry Ransom Humanities Research Center, University of Texas, Austin. Yet as the only extended fiction (apart from another film treatment) which Greene wrote between *The Third Man* and *The End of the Affair*, it represents an important link between those two works both technically and thematically, acting as something of a sequel to the former and a 'prequel' to the latter. Moreover, various neglected archival materials dating from early 1950 and centring on the composition of *No Man's Land* illuminate a fascinating, if brief, period of creative activity which coincided with a critical stage in his emotionally turbulent affair with Catherine Walston. The American-born wife of the wealthy farmer and politician Henry (Harry) Walston, later Lord Walston, she was the model for both Clara in *No Man's Land* and Sarah Miles in *The End of the Affair*. Their liaison began in 1947 and lasted roughly thirteen years. Greene made her a director of his newly formed film and production company in 1950, gaining some satisfaction from the fact that if she would not consent to be his marriage partner, she was at least his business partner.

Shortly after their successful collaboration on *The Third Man*, Graham Greene wrote a memo to his agent, Laurence Pollinger, outlining a plan for a further film venture with film producer Alexander Korda and the director Carol Reed:

I had dinner with Korda and Carol Reed last night, January 11th [1950], and sketched an idea for a film to take place in the Harz Mountains. The main themes are the security measures taken by the Russians against information on the uranium workings and the presence of a kind of Teresa Neumann character who attracts religious pilgrims from outside the area. I suggested that the film should open with some very quiet pastoral countryside and the arrival of pilgrims either at the house of the visionary or at some shrine. For several minutes the audience imagines this is going to be a quiet pastoral piece when one of the pilgrims makes some odd slip which discloses that his or her presence with the pilgrims is not a genuine one. [Unpublished letter, dated 12th January 1950, in Harry Ransom Humanities Research Center, University of Texas, Austin.]

Korda duly commissioned Greene to provide a prose treatment for what was tentatively referred to as 'The Harz Mountains Story'. The 'untrammelled publishing rights of the story' were to be Greene's; the film rights were to be owned by Korda's London Films Productions Ltd. An early journalistic reference to the proposed film appeared in 'Looking Ahead in the Film World' in the Exeter *Express and Echo* newspaper on 8th March 1950. Its author notes that a third collaboration between Reed and Greene was under way, with Greene already at work on the screenplay in America, 'where he is supervising production of the dramatisation of his novel *The Heart of the Matter*...' No details are announced beyond the fact that it will be a modern drama set in post-war Germany. 'But this much I can say,' adds Reed. 'It won't be a suspense thriller, and it won't be in the least like *The Third Man*. And there'll be no zither music either.' Apparently Reed planned on casting James Mason in the lead role, and three weeks after this interview,

Reed cabled Greene, who was by then registered in the Hotel Klause in Goslar, the chief town of the Harz Mountains area, and already 4,500 words into the draft, telling him that Greta Garbo was 'very interested'. (It is unclear why Reed discussed *No Man's Land* with Garbo. She would have been forty-four at this time and had been inactive in films for several years. Clara is only thirty.) By 3rd April 1950, London's *Daily Herald* had published a brief item with the title 'Expect a Spectre', referring to Greene's visit to the Harz, where he was planning to 'make a film there based on the East-West tensions'. The newspaper report also refers to a spectre which allegedly appears on the 3,700-foot Brocken summit – the mountain featured in Goethe's *Faust* – every 1st May (Walpurgis night). Greene, initially at least, seemed to envision the presence in his story of a character based on Teresa Neumann, the famous German mystic and stigmatist, as the object of pilgrimage, but later changed that aspect of the story in favour of a visitation from the Virgin herself, who appears, holding a rose, to two children, in an area that has recently come under the control of the Russian occupying forces. To Greene's perturbation, the publicity from the newspaper story led to a steady stream of unwanted visitors to his Goslar hotel. Early in April the *Daily Mail* correspondent filed a report entitled, 'Paging Meester Greene':

> ...He is there for ten days, gathering material for another 'Third Man' film, based on the army of the homeless who daily cross over from the Soviet zone. But so far work has been held up by this constant stream of Germans trying to foist onto him every sort of 'anti' story – anti-Russian, anti-British, anti-Western Allied, anti-Socialist. 'Anyway,' Greene told me... 'the film which Carol Reed and I will shoot in the enchanting Harz Mountains will be entirely non-political. We shall tell only in terms of human

experience and suffering the story of Germany's eight million refugees.'

Since Reed's misgivings about merely repeating his success with *The Third Man* clashed with Greene's decision to write a suspense-thriller with many of the elements of Reed's recent award-winning film, it is not surprising that the project came to nothing. Moreover, not only was Greene distracted from his writing task by demanding journalists, but he was much more interested in gaining a greater percentage of his mistress' affections than in writing fiction. He seems to have been aware that while he was in Germany, Catherine was seeing an American military officer, and he was also aware that Catherine was spending disconcertingly large amounts of her time measuring curtains and carpets in preparation for a residential move with her husband into a lavish mansion at Newton Hall, a 25-bedroom house near Thriplow Farm in Cambridgeshire. In Greene's words, he feared the descent of an 'iron curtain' between Catherine and himself. As William Cash puts it, in his book *The Third Woman*, at this time Greene felt he was losing her:

> Always lurking in the back of his mind was Catherine's impending move from Thriplow Farm to the stately grandeur of Newton Hall... If she was to leave her husband, Greene knew... it was not going to be just as she had installed herself as the chatelaine of a vast... mansion... almost like the Ritz.

Little wonder Greene's letters were full of remorse for his recent jealousies and protestations of desperate love, coupled at times with a stated desire for death if he could not have her to himself. Greene's letters of March–April 1950 to Catherine Walston give a kind of day-by-day progress report as he struggled to complete 'this beastly story', for 'the sooner I'm through... the sooner I'll see you.' Although the film project was abortive, the recent availability of archival material at Georgetown University's Lauinger Library, combined with the presence of a 'Harz Mountains Film' folder in the Greene Papers at the Burns Special Collections Library of Boston College, means it is now possible to get an uncommon insight into Greene's creative process, as he kept a kind of diary during his roughly two-week sojourn in the region, soaking up background information that would be used in the story.

For example, the comic scene in which the protagonist, Richard Brown, walks out of an amateur drama festival owes its existence in the text to Greene's own perfunctory attendance at a military dramatic competition to which his Foreign Office contact in Bünde had brought him. In one of the many letters from Goslar (3rd April 1950), he announced to Catherine that his attendance would at least provide a comic episode for the story, and Greene uses the amateur theatrical competition at the beginning and the end as a kind of image of uneventful normality, the return to which signals closure from the thriller aspect of his tale. Boundary Inspector Parnell also provided Greene with a bogus cover as his assistant, allowing him to visit the Russian zone on Tuesday 4th April 1950 without attracting unwanted attention. Before meeting Parnell, Greene had also reconnoitred with Colonel Harold Gibson ('Gibbie'), someone he referred to as a member of 'the old firm'; in other words, one involved in espionage. In fact, Gibson had been head of the Secret Intelligence Service (SIS) station in Prague just before the War, and shortly after the War he returned there. Two months after Greene met with him in Bünde, Gibson was named as a conspirator in a failed attempt to overthrow the Communist Czech Government. Perhaps Greene obtained some of his details about espionage in the Harz region from 'Gibbie'.

The 'Harz Mountains' file, now at Boston College, which Greene kept during the planning stages of the film, contains numerous cuttings relevant to his assignment. A leading article from *The Times*, 27th January 1950, is particularly significant. Headed 'The Hydrogen Bomb', it goes on to discuss the recently discovered 'New Method of Releasing Energy for Destruction', and after describing the importance of Uranium 235 in the process, it ends with the chilling words that 'within... a few years it will be possible for any Power with modern industrial resources to destroy the world as we know it.' Clearly Greene wanted to exploit the disturbing implications of the recent uranium discoveries at Eisleben in the Soviet zone. Indeed, as early as 23rd January 1950, Greene writes to Korda, saying: 'I gather from John Codrington that he is producing the right man for me to talk to about uranium this afternoon. The story is growing quite nicely under the surface,' but he argued that the actual writing would be better commenced after his arrival in Germany so that the on-site impressions would be more vivid. But evidently Greene was mustering plot details as early as January 1950.

The same file at Boston College contains a cutting from the *Manchester Guardian*, apparently a gift from Greene's brother Hugh. Headed 'How "Confessions" Are Secured in the Iron Curtain Countries', the story recounts the harrowing experiences of a former translator at the United States Legation in Sofia, who, after long hours of brutal interrogation at the hands of the secret police, offered a confession. At the not-quite-halfway point, Greene obviously incorporates into his text that graphically detailed description of the method used to extract the confession: the prisoner is forced to support his weight on two fingers while leaning against a wall for six hours.

The parallels to *The Third Man* are clear, and they might even account for Reed's decision to proceed no further with the project. From England, on 19th April, Greene wrote to Colonel Gibson: 'To my relief Carol did not like the story in its present form and we are not going ahead at all with the subject until after I have had my holiday [the holiday in Italy he was so eagerly expecting to share in May with Catherine Walston].' It, too, is set in occupied war zones, and its narrator, Redburn, is also a military official who resembles Calloway in *The Third Man*. Furthermore, the antagonist, Starhov – like Harry Lime – has an emotional hold over the heroine; both see to it that the beautiful refugees – Anna Schmidt in *The Third Man*, and Clara in *No Man's Land* – can escape relocation and certain imprisonment within the Eastern bloc. Moreover, just as Martins has a strong bond with Lime, so too does Brown forge a trusting relationship with the Turgenev-loving Starhov. And, despite Greene's puzzled response to a report that the Russians were angered over his depiction of them in *The Third Man*, his portrayal of them in *No Man's Land* is only slightly less negative. Only the Russians, it would seem, ever resort to the physical abuse of prisoners.

Readers of *No Man's Land* might be surprised to encounter Greene's evident debt to Ivan Turgenev, not only in his several allusions within the text to Turgenev's stories and plays, such as *On the Eve*, *A Lear of the Steppes* and *A Month in the Country*. It was Greene's habit to read while travelling, and in a letter to Catherine Walston during his stay in Goslar, he mentions that he is currently reading Turgenev's *On the Eve*, and in another, recommends *A Lear of the Steppes* to Catherine: 'how good it is... do read it.' So, not surprisingly, Greene borrows the necessary Slavic names from the Russian author he has just been rereading. But Greene's further debt to Turgenev lies in characterisation. Greene appropriates the name Starhov, with a minor adaptation, for his own text (Turgenev's Stahov is the libertine father in *On the Eve*). Greene's Starhov closely resembles Turgenev's idealistic Bulgarian patriot Insarov. Like Insarov, a central character in *On the Eve*, Greene's Starhov ultimately puts his trust in his country rather than his mistress. Finally, Greene's hitherto unnoticed affection for Turgenev leads him to use the great Russian author as a symbol of an Arcadian past, whose verbal landscapes contrast so palpably with those of the Harz region, a region which, since Goethe's *Faust*, had been associated with the darker aspects of nature, but which, since its post-war division into hostile boundaries, conjured up even more sinister associations. Greene paints similar polarities in his wartime novel, *The Ministry of Fear*. Arthur Rowe's memories of an idyllic past conflict with his stark descriptions of a perilous and evil present. Turgenev's world is now very different from that served by MI6 and the KGB. His rich pastoral landscapes, cited by Starhov in *No Man's Land*, contrast strikingly with the violent present of Greene's Cold-War Europe:

> This isn't real life any more... Tea on the lawn, evensong, croquet, the old ladies calling, the gentle, unmalicious gossip, the gardener trundling the wheelbarrow full of leaves and grass... it's not there any more... You used to laugh at the books... about spies, and murders, and violence... The world has been remade by William Le Queux. [*The Ministry of Fear*]

If Le Queux, an Edwardian writer of popular spy thrillers, stands for the age of anxiety, then Turgenev represents for Greene an age of peace. And in 1950 Greene desperately longed for peace. Time and again in Greene's letters and poems of 1949–50 to Catherine, he associates her with peace. On 3rd March 1950, before arriving in Germany, he speaks of a need for a 'peaceful week' with Catherine before a turf fire – or perhaps she could accompany him to Germany? But he preferred the prospect of returning with

Catherine to Achill, the site of her rented cottage in Ireland, where the pair had spent an idyllic holiday together early in their relationship. From Goslar on 31st March he writes to her of 'the peace we have so often', and on 3rd April he says, 'Now one wants peace.' The day before, he tells Catherine of a walk he took along the East German border and being invited by an armed policeman to 'step over – and one half-longed to: one wants you or disappearance.' In a sense, Greene projects his own fatigue and desire for peace onto Starhov, and his jealousy onto Brown. Throughout the text, Starhov succumbs to sleep; then, finally, he disappears. On the other hand, Brown wins the girl, but he will remain 'hopelessly insecure because the whole world must want' the first beautiful woman he has ever loved.

An important link between *No Man's Land* and the novel he was working on at the same time, *The End of the Affair* (begun in 1949), is the theme of jealousy and trust. Norman Sherry, in the second volume of his *Life of Graham Greene*, reports that at this time Catherine Walston was having an affair with Lowell Weicker, Sr., the wealthy president of the E.R. Squibb Pharmaceutical Company, and her behaviour during the spring of 1950 had seemingly turned Greene into a jealous wreck. Just as Brown, at the end of *No Man's Land*, is likely to be haunted by visions of the green-eyed monster, so too does Bendrix in *The End of the Affair* refer to the pangs of jealousy: 'I'd rather be dead or see you dead… than with another man. I'm not eccentric. That's ordinary human love.' Even when Brown succeeds in persuading Clara to marry him – something Greene failed to do with Catherine – his reaction is very unlike joy, and when Bendrix first makes love to his conquest Sarah, his reaction is similar: 'I went home that first evening with no exhilaration, but only a sense of sadness and resignation… that I was only one of many men – the favourite lover for the moment.'

Greene's letters from Germany suggest that his own behaviour parallels that of Bendrix as he describes his jealous courtship of Sarah. Fanning himself into 'anger or remorse', Bendrix believes that he was 'forcing the pace... I was pushing... the only thing I loved out of my life.'

Perhaps Greene's insecurity with respect to Catherine sprang in part from a realisation that he was acting in much the same way. On 27th March, he writes:

> I feel such fear of losing you through my own stupidity... Tomorrow I begin the wretched story... but except when I'm with you I seem to have lost not only the pleasure in writing, but my resilience in words: I have more important things in my mind now than fictional words. Marry me, Catherine... How many times one writes the same words till they must be stale as dry bread to you, but never has one conceived the possibility of loving so completely... I'll never leave you unless you ask me to.

Confronting Henry Miles with his assessment of why he thinks Sarah left him, Bendrix says, 'I wanted love to go on and on, never to get less...' He believes that his insistence on a *permanent* love and on her leaving her husband, coupled with his jealousies and anger, drove her away. 'I became a bore and a fool too.'

Familiarity with the love letters to Catherine gives the reader a better understanding of why Greene focuses on jealousy and betrayal in *The Third Man*, *No Man's Land* and *The End of the Affair*. Arguably too dependent on coincidence in one major scene, and perhaps weakened by one implausible detail in the climactic scene; nevertheless, the story rises above these flaws. Greene's nose for atmosphere and eye for detail are as acute as ever. For example, in one deft phrase, 'on the Nordhausen road', he conveys the horror of the holocaust – the network of subterranean forced labour camps of Dora-Mittelbau, which, along with his description of the refugee who falls among thieves, says so much about the modern wasteland. Other touches serve a lighter purpose: by contrasting the chase scenes with descriptions of mundane army canteens, and ersatz alpine Swiss architecture, he heightens their urgency.

At the risk of echoing Greene's too-easily impressed drama festival adjudicator, characterisation is, indeed, 'excellent'. Although it would be easy enough to turn the work into a modern-day exemplum, with the three principals embodying abstract ideas – Clara, Christian charity; Brown, despair; and Starhov, ideology – the characters transcend the allegorical through the complexity of their responses. As a link between two of his major works, its place in the Greene canon is long overdue.

Unlike *No Man's Land*, Greene's unfinished film treatment, *The Stranger's Hand* was eventually filmed, although Greene's authorial contribution was apparently limited to the first 15,000 words as reproduced in this volume. And although the final typescript, which runs to a length of seventy-three legal-sized pages and is now housed in the Graham Greene archive at Boston College, credits Greene on the title page as the sole author, the treatment was, in fact, completed by veteran screenwriter Guy Elmes with Greene's approval. For box-office reasons, Elmes promptly substituted a female character, Roberta, a hotel chambermaid, for Greene's original character, Roberto, the hotel waiter who befriends the young protagonist Roger Court.

The 1954 film was funded by Alexander Korda, directed by Greene's friend Mario Soldati and featured two of the principal actors in *The Third Man*: Trevor Howard in the role of Major Court, Roger's policeman father, and Alida Valli as the female lead, Roberta. Why a British national should be serving as a Major in the Venezia-Giulia police is clear: seized by the Germans in 1943, Trieste was occupied by Tito's forces in 1945, and claimed for Yugoslavia. However, the Treaty of Paris created a Free Territory of Trieste, guaranteed by the United Nations Security Council. The territory was divided into two zones. Zone A was administered by British and American forces. Zone B was given to Yugoslavia. This division proved unworkable, and in 1954 Trieste was granted to Italy, and most of the rest of Zone A and all of Zone B to Yugoslavia. So *The Stranger's Hand*, like the two previous film stories Greene wrote for Korda – *The Third Man* and *No Man's Land* – was set in disputed territory.

Greene's draft concludes as Major Court and Peskovitch, the Istrian patriot now a dangerous enemy of Tito's, are being transferred after their kidnapping in Venice to a Yugoslavian freighter which will bring the pair behind the Iron Curtain. Joe Hamstringer, Roberta's boyfriend, familiar with the Venetian dock area because of his black-market dealings, correctly guesses that the pair might be on the Yugoslavian ship and goes aboard for a talk with the ship's steward. Hamstringer sets a fire in the ship so that the Italian authorities, whose fireboats have surrounded the ship, can legally come aboard. A gun battle ensues, and just as Court and Peskovitch are about to be murdered in their cabin by a Communist guard, the doctor who had drugged the captives tries to stop the gunman and, in the ensuing mêlée, is killed by the bullet meant for them. In the final scene, Major Court and Peskovitch are rescued by the Venetian police, and Roger Court is reunited with his father.

– *James Sexton, 2005*

Acknowledgements

I wish to thank the Social Sciences and Humanities Research Council of Canada for a travel grant that helped make this edition possible. John Atteberry of the John J. Burns Library, Boston College; Marty Barringer of the Lauinger Library, Georgetown University; and Tara Wenger of the Harry Ransom Humanities Research Center, University of Texas, Austin, all provided cordial and timely assistance. The following scholars all shared their expertise: Hugh Aplin, Perry Biddiscombe, Geoffrey Hargreaves and David Stafford. Throughout the entire publishing process, Hesperus Press's editors have provided exemplary support. Lastly, I wish to thank my wife, Janice, for her ongoing support.

No Man's Land

Chapter one

I had noticed him for days in the club restaurant sitting there in the same spot, always alone with a book propped in front of him: a man in the early forties with an expression of tired patience as though his life were spent waiting around in such unrewarding spots as the leave-centre of Braunlage.[1] He was surrounded by the angular discontented faces of the occupying wives who would come in on a few days' leave, sometimes with their husbands and sometimes in small hen parties with no other object than inspecting a NAAFI[2] shop – nylon stockings, a few scarves, some Molineux scent, gloves, a selection of bad children's books. It wasn't the skiing season, so they came and went rapidly, while he stayed on, a civilian with a book. I wondered sometimes whether he was waiting for a girl to join him, but surely then there would have been some signs of impatience, and of that I could never have accused him.

Once I met him walking in the forest alone. Even then he had his book with him, stuck in his pocket. We were a couple of kilometres east of Braunlage, and I thought it just as well to have a word with him, so I said, 'Good afternoon,' and fell into step. He was perfectly polite: nobody could ever have said that he resented his solitude being broken – even the army wives had nothing to complain of: he was just neutral, that was all.

I said, 'The paths here are a bit tricky. Have you a compass?'

'Oh,' he said, 'I don't go far enough to need a compass.'

'My name's Redburn of the Boundary Inspection.'

'My name's Brown,' he said, 'Richard Brown' – even his name was neutral.

'Control Commission?'

'No. Just a holiday. Spending my fifty pounds.'

'All alone?'

'I'm expecting a friend any day.'

'You want to be careful if you walk much.'

'Careful?'

'Not to lose your way. We are only a kilometre from the Russian zone.'[3]

He gave me back an annoying smile. 'Ah, the famous Iron Curtain.'

'It's a stupid phrase,' I said, 'even if the Great Man did invent it.[4] There'd be no difficulty if the curtain were really iron, but it's like any other curtain – you can push your way through, only it has so many folds and you can easily get lost in the folds.'

'Yes,' he said, 'they can hardly patrol these hills properly.' The trees stretched all round us as regular as pillars, a vast hall of pillars – one could see no doorway anywhere. 'I suppose I'd better go along down,' he said.

'That way?'

'No, that way.'

I didn't see Brown for a good many days after that. We were having a certain amount of trouble on the Boundary Inspection Service because of a vision – yes, a vision, it was as simple and as absurd as that. The vision had taken place – taken root would be the fitter phrase – during one of the dark days of the War. The Harz is staunchly Protestant, but in a village called Ilsenhof there were enough Catholics to maintain a church. Protestants don't go in for visions, though of course in the old days in these parts they went in for witches, and in the shops at Goslar you can buy little old ladies in spectacles and poke bonnets mounted on broomsticks. But this wasn't a witch, it was the Virgin herself who appeared to a couple of children at the entrance of a natural cave outside Ilsenhof.[5] It was winter – the first snow had fallen – and she gave the children a rose. That was the one inexplicable part of the story – and so personally I disbelieve it. I am a busy man in a position of some authority and I have no room in my life for the inexplicable, but oh, what a nuisance it can be. Within a few months Ilsenhof was a centre of pilgrimage. People would walk from as far as Catholic Bavaria; they would come from the other side of the Weser; even Czechoslovakia sent its pilgrims; and when the War was over, it became an allied problem. The village was first of all in the British zone, but in readjusting the zones and eliminating an enclave, the village became several kilometres inside Russian territory. The Catholics were indignant, though I should have thought if they had faith in this vision they would have been glad to see it planted in the enemy soil, but one could hardly alter geography all over again for the sake of what two children said they had seen nearly ten years ago. The local Russian command, of course, we assumed, would simply abolish it. The sound of an explosion in the hills started a rumour that the cave had been dynamited, but you always have to treat most anti-Russian stories with reserve, for six months later the pilgrimages were on again. If the Russian Commander had really objected, he had been overruled by someone.

It was a tricky position for the Russians. New uranium deposits had been found around Eisleben in the Harz area, and there was an obvious clash between the requirements of propaganda and security. For the sake of propaganda and for the sake, too, of a contented population (for even the Protestants had developed a local pride in the Virgin of Ilsenhof) the Russians would have liked to leave the pilgrimage intact, all the more so perhaps because of the dark rumours that centred round the Czech uranium mines. Forced labour after all is not in the long run as good as free labour – or shall we say controlled labour?

Propaganda apparently won for the time being, but the pilgrimage, I should imagine, must have suffered a good deal in commercial value; you would have to be very religious indeed, or very ignorant before you entered the Russian zone for the sake of somebody else's vision. Certain roads were allotted to the pilgrims and special passes given them, and this gave my office a good deal of work. I sometimes wished we could close the pilgrimage from our side, but the democracies could hardly show themselves less tolerant than the Russians. *Their* tolerance caused an immense amount of friction – some people holding proper passes would be turned back, some would be admitted without passes at all, and there were always rumours of people who never returned. At one time the story was spread that a whole pilgrimage had been sent to the uranium mines – there wasn't a word of truth in it, of course.

Then one afternoon I got word from the German frontier patrol that one of my countrymen was down by the block on the Nordhausen road with no apparent object, and I drove there to look at him. Beyond Braunlage the frontier of the Russian zone approaches nearer and nearer to the highway. By the time you reach the village of Hohengeisse, the frontier is just across a few yards of ground spotted with the sawn trunks of trees like a battleground. Beyond the village, on the road to Nordhausen, where they used to make the best *Schnapps* in Germany until the town disappeared into the mysterious region of 'over there', the left-hand ditch is Russian, the right British. I never feel quite at my ease on those three kilometres (one of our officers was shot there last year 'accidentally'), with the thick woods on either side, where the East and the West patrols work through the shadows, looking for smugglers or deserters. A frontier sign, a notice announcing the roadblock and then the block itself, just a few tree trunks, a tangle of brown twigs, the rusty radiator of an old car, twenty yards of no man's land, and then the other boundary post and a crossroads lying wide open and the sense of an unfathomable emptiness that the propagandists of two worlds have imposed on our minds.

Brown stood there looking across the block to the little group of East German police in their blue uniforms and a single Russian soldier in green khaki who, for some reason, had his arms full of grass. A frontier patrol with his rifle unslung watched Brown from our side of the road, and the East German police waved to him and called out to him that the road was open on their side and invited him to climb across the barrier. An old car drew up beside them and the driver watched too, and the empty road behind them ran on towards Nordhausen and Asia.

'Good afternoon, Brown,' I said. 'Want anything?'

'No, oh no, nothing.'

'You look as if you had an appointment.'

He smiled. 'Oh no, just curiosity.'

'I wouldn't trust them too far.'

'There is something strange and sad, isn't there, about a no man's land – even when there's only twenty yards of it. A place on this earth where nobody can ever build or sleep.' He looked at the trees on the Russian side. 'Is that no man's land too?'

'No, that's Russian. I'm not sure whether they claim the ditch you're standing in.'

He said, 'They don't put up any wire.'

'No. I told you it's not an iron curtain.'

'Well, I'd better be getting back.'

'Have you got a car somewhere?'

'No, I've walked. Began to feel the need of exercise, you know, sitting around.'

'Your friend hasn't turned up?'

'No.'

'Overdue?' I don't know what made me use a term more applicable to a lost ship than a lost appointment. He hesitated and said, 'I expect him any day,' and his voice, like a wireless operator forced against his will by a revolver at his back, sent out an involuntary signal of anxiety and distress.

Why should a civilian called Brown have so weighed on my mind? God knows, I had plenty to do. There was, for one example, the question of the Polish refugees. We had agreed to accept twenty-five thousand of them in the British zone and now the Russians were rumoured to be sending a quarter of a million. They began to arrive by train and we couldn't shunt them back, walking cases, stretcher cases without stretchers – and the bodies – there were quite a number of bodies. And there was the murder near Walkenried, a shocking murder however used one had got to shocks in the last four years. Three smugglers had agreed to convoy a German over the demarcation line. He had a family in the Russian zone and he was carrying two suitcases when, in the railway station at Walkenried, the smugglers spotted him. They told him of the trouble he would have at the frontier and he agreed to set out with them in the darkness over the mountain. No Walpurgisnacht on the Brocken can have contained quite so much horror as that scene when they halted and beat him on the head. He wouldn't stop screaming, so they bludgeoned him again. But he was still able to get on his knees to pray for mercy and the leader crammed his victim's scarf into his mouth and thrust it further and further down his throat with a walking stick until he died – there is a photograph on the police files of the dead face and the dribble of scarf out of the mouth. We know what happened because one of the men gave himself up.

I only mention these things because such incidents are the background to a frontier life. Who was it who said, 'The world has been abandoned into the hands of men?...'[6] It certainly seemed true in that year on that particular border. Occasionally I found myself envying those who could believe in a winter Virgin carrying a rose. Brown was waiting for I don't know whom, and I was waiting for I don't know what. So was a whole occupying army, and with what absurdities we tried to occupy ourselves while we waited. That too is part of the background.

The Combined Forces and the Control Commission were holding their annual Drama Festival at Bad Harzburg. Every night three one-act plays were staged before a suave patronising judge fetched out from the Academy of Dramatic Art in London and an audience filled with a kind of stifling goodwill. It took one back to the old days of school where any serious criticism in the magazine would have seemed like a breach of tact because it would have discouraged the boys. At the end of the evening the judge came forward and commented on the individual productions. 'Now the Herford Club – that was a really good production, excellent characterisation, and the way the door kept on blowing open – that really did admirably convey the effect of a storm. Then the Goslar Club – really good character-isation here, excellent production. You really felt the producer knew what he was after. The visitors from Frankfurt – very intel-ligent choice of play. Admirable characterisation. I'd like to congratulate the producer on that little bit of business with a cigarette lighter...'

In the interval between the first and second play, as though inevitably now, I picked out from all those rows of officers and wives the face of Brown, sitting there, talking to nobody, though one of his military or official neighbours, I suppose, must have invited him or he could hardly have got in. I had noticed him first because he was always in the same place at the same time, and for that reason he gave an effect of patience: now that he was, as it were, continually cropping up he conveyed the sense of restlessness, as though he had come to an end of patience and was roaming a room, from wall to wall and back again. I felt that he would ultimately open a door and walk out, and that was exactly what he did.

The second play was an extraordinary piece of 'ham' found in God knows what paper-covered collection of plays suited to amateurs. It was called 'The Lordship of the Sea' and it was about a family of fishermen called the Combers who would come striding in to hang up oilskins, swallow some tea, make trenchant remarks about 'there's always been a Comber in the lifeboat', and dash out again to drown one by one, while the mother and the sisters watched with dour approval, and sweethearts tried to lure the Combers to inland graves. Clouds rushed across the backcloth, thunder clanged like iron and the Combers shouted passionately and fraternally, 'As long as there's a Comber alive, that old devil, that old devil, the sea...' I heard a slight disturbance behind me and, looking back, saw Brown making for the exit. RASC[7] officers in mess kit stared rigidly at the stage, but their wives were obviously disturbed by Brown's breach of taste: even the actors noticed his persistent and long-drawn-out exit down the row and fumbled their lines.

I felt great sympathy with Brown, but I hadn't his courage – or was it, as one of the wives suggested later, just ignorance? A great deal that happened was due to his ignorance. Though it was a long time before I heard and put together the details of what happened to him when the night took him out of earshot of the last Combers. I suppose the third play of the evening – a bonhomous piece of optimism and goodwill by Priestley[8] – had just started and we had put Brown right out of mind just about the time he entered the Russian zone. What followed is reasonably accurate. Unhappy people confide even in strangers.

Chapter two

Bad Harzburg is a rather ugly spa town that straggles from the valley up the slopes of the foothills. The Teutonic houses try unsuccessfully to recall the fancifulness of Swiss architecture, but yellow beams turn liverish and scarlet-maroon, and the fir trees that come down the hills towards the houses are like fellow-actors who have also not mastered the atmosphere, an atmosphere that depends after all on more than a century of peace. There are no zones in Switzerland. There is no need to indicate on tree stumps the approach of a border. Brown had only three kilometres to go.

If he had known his way about he couldn't have chosen a better point to cross. Smugglers operate further from British centres and the German patrols are less dense here than in the area around Braunlage. Smugglers are human too, and they prefer the less mountainous routes. Brown had some stiff climbing to do in the dark before he reached the frontier.

There were no incidents at all. Once he lost his footing on a tree trunk bridging a little rapid mountain stream and went in up to his knees: once he thought he saw a border patrol standing with unslung rifle awaiting his approach, and after a long pause he went forward in an attitude of surrender, hands above his head, to greet a tree split by some last-year's lightning flash. He went forward from one zone into the next unchallenged. The curtain opened at a touch to receive him into its folds.

When he was certain that he had left the British zone right behind, he lay down in some underbrush and slept, slept as he hadn't slept for a week. He told somebody later, 'You see I was at peace. I was doing something. I wasn't waiting any more.' When he woke it was broad daylight and from the edge of the trees he looked down at a waste of almost empty fields (one man was burning leaves a long way off) and the roofs of a village. There was nothing to tell him except the sun that he was looking east and not west: there was nothing sinister any longer now that the roadblock had been crossed. It was like the peace that follows an interrogation.

In the village he made a bad mistake. He went into a shop to buy some bread and offered his Western marks in exchange. The woman held them in her hand and looked at them and at once he remembered the difference in currency. There was nothing to do except wait patiently for the next move. She said, '*Sie kommen aus dem Westen*?' '*Ja*.' The notes lay in the palm of her hand like an exhibit in court. She said nothing. She was looking over his shoulder at the street behind. He turned and looked too. A car had drawn up. There was something wrong about the car and it was a moment before he realised what was wrong – it was a good car, that was all, an expensive car, a well-groomed car, in fact a Mercedes. He turned back to the woman and held out his hand – whether to take the notes back or to appeal to her, he could not have said. The car lay like a watchdog across the doorway. He watched the worn eyes of the shop woman shift this way and that, and he thought '*Finis*, it's *finis*.' Then suddenly her fist closed on the notes and put them out of sight, and a woman's voice asked for bread.

He described it later – and my informant told me that for some reason we neither of us then understood that he spoke with asperity or perhaps bitterness. 'I was tired, you see, and scared and there she stood quite humbly, waiting for her bread. It was only a small village – I didn't even know its name and she was beautiful, she even had a good suit on that might have come from Dior. You don't expect a beautiful woman in a small village, do you, and she was more beautiful than you'd expect in a whole world of women. I tell you I was tired and scared: perhaps at an Embassy cocktail party, talking about the opera or the books she had been reading lately, it wouldn't have had any effect on me, but as it was, I loved her. It was as simple as that. They say the young fall in love at first sight. Perhaps it's the middle-aged. We haven't time to lose. And the baker's woman thrust the goods across to her as if she were mud and she took them and went back to her Mercedes and drove away.'

'Yes, and then?' my informant asked.

Brown told him with a kind of disgust, 'Oh then, all the worry began. You see then I wanted to finish, to get out, to live.'

* * *

When the car had driven away, the baker's wife opened her hand. Brown wanted to ask her who the woman was, but what was the good? In a car like that the roads were open as far as Moscow: there were no roadblocks to the East. She had most of Europe to be lost in.

The woman said, 'Come inside,' and he followed her.

'Have you any more of this?' she asked him. He emptied his pockets of notes; they were no longer any good to him. He kept a few BAFs[9] for luck: British army currency was no good to him here, it might be a danger, but one had to assume that one day one would be going back. He watched her take the money, put it in a drawer and lock it. Then she counted out the equivalent number of Eastern marks. He was impressed and grateful; only later did it occur to him that she had made a very good deal for herself, since every Western mark was worth at least seven Eastern.

'It is good of you,' he said, and was about to leave the shop when she reminded him that he hadn't paid for the bread. Again he was on the point of leaving when it occurred to him that there was no reason not to trust her a little further. He took out of his wallet the photograph of a man some ten years younger than himself: an amused tough face with a scar from the corner of the left eye running down towards the mouth.

'Have you seen anyone like that around here?' She shook her head, wasting no words on him, as though she compromised herself less that way.

He said, 'Which is the road to Ilsenhof?'

'Turn right. There is a signpost.'

'Is it far?'

'No.'

She might have told him how many kilometres, he thought, but I suppose she had no breath to waste, since the big yellow sign soon told him that. Four kilometres – one had only to walk down the road. There was nobody at all in sight, and he felt expected, under observation, walking down the long straight way, pale with dust. He wondered whether the Mercedes car had driven that road ahead of him. It was odd, disturbing, rather sad being interested in an unknown woman again – almost antique, pre-war.

As he approached Ilsenhof the road became less deserted. Small knots of dark-clothed elderly people came out onto it from the side roads, a crowded bus went hooting by – he was reminded of the approach to a not very important fair ground. But there were still no police. He had not seen a single frontier patrol since he crossed the border. Man is difficult to satisfy. He had heard so much of a thing called the police state that he was worried by their absence: he was reminded of those men who had waved to him from the other side of the roadblock, smiling, encouraging...

There must have been about fifty people on the road ahead of him now, and he could see below in the valley the red sloping roofs of Ilsenhof. He stopped and tore a piece of bread off his loaf: he noticed that his hand trembled when it went to his mouth. He wondered what plays they would be doing at the drama festival that night: was it possible that he could still do what he had to and be back by curtain rise?

On the right twenty yards ahead a path ran up into the forest. In a miniature penthouse at the foot of the path Christ dangled upon a cross. All the way up the path, small noticeboards (he couldn't see the writing on them) hung from the tree, like notices to trespassers. But if that was what they were, there were plenty of trespassers – all but one of the people ahead of him turned up the path. Brown went on down the road to Ilsenhof.

It would have been like any other village he had seen in the Western zone (except that the shops were nearly empty, and outside what might have been once the *Rathaus* a large board proclaimed the headquarters of the local Communist party) if it hadn't been for a strange ribbon development along the way east of the town. A row of ugly villas looked as though they had been run up almost overnight by people who had not intended to stay – it was like a boom town in a mining area, but the boom had passed on. A window full of holy junk caught Brown's eye – bad plaster images of a Virgin carrying a rose, always the same Virgin and the same attitude, turned out by the hundreds in a factory, at Dresden probably; cheap rosaries, boxes full of holy medals, picture postcards of a grotto taken in a bad light, some imaginary scenes in the worst possible taste of two children kneeling in the snow before this vision with a rose. Over all the contents of the shop was a feeling difficult to define of dust and unchangeableness: you felt that everything had come from the factory a long time ago. Brown entered.

A very old woman emerged from the parlour behind and stared at him with hostility and suspicion: Brown wondered whether he carried his scepticism on his clothes like a badge. He chose a holy medal and paid for it, a sense of guilt growing under her unwinking gaze. He said in German, 'Have you by any chance?...' but whatever question he was going to ask wilted before her suspicion. She put her hand under the counter and pulled out a pair of steel-rimmed spectacles and put them on to see him better: then she thrust out at him a second box of medals identical with the last.

He was daunted by her and against his own will he ran his fingers through the junk – one would believe if one could, in visions and eternal love, but he wasn't here for that. There were not only medals in the box, there were hideous paper knives bearing the pious painted image; knives with liturgical inscriptions; even a cigarette case with a picture of the grotto on the lid; buttons in the shape of the miraculous rose, but again he felt that nobody had looked at these objects for a very long while. Perhaps he ought to buy one more medal in order to get away, but did Catholics carry two medals? It was the kind of fact he should have known and checked like a military flash. He lifted up the cigarette case and saw there, half hidden among the medals, a knife... He found his heart pounding and his hand was unsteady again as it reached in the box. He thought: it's not possible, not possible that on the other side of the knife I shall find my own initials, R.B. He would have liked to walk straight out, back to the woods, back to the stream, the shattered tree, the ugly houses on the other side before the despair struck. He picked the knife out of the tray and there the initials were, almost obliterated, etched awkwardly in by a boy thirty years ago with the help of a chemical outfit, and the woods and the stream and the tree seemed out of reach for ever.

* * *

He couldn't understand the singing any more than he had understood the holy medals and the statues, and the postcard booth at the first halt on the path where the Stations of the Cross began. They too were in the worst possible taste – the fervour of the old women jabbering their prayers and moving on in their high black boots was ugly to him. At the second halt a cripple was selling candles, and though Brown pretended to be engaged in prayer, this didn't prevent the man from pestering him until simply for the sake of peace he bought and carried his candle with all the others up the steep path to the grotto, from which the singing came. He thought how can a faith survive this?

Or this? he thought, kneeling with a hundred others at the mouth of the cave, where the same hideous image magnified six times held out the rose towards them, and the priest moving from this side to the other of the altar said his mass. The walls of the cave were hung with cheap replicas of hearts and legs and even human kidneys, and he remembered how with more dignity in Horace's Ode the fishermen had hung out their nets at the shrine of Venus.[10] How right the Russians were to leave this – thing, these rites, an exhibition of the absurdities of faith. While the others prayed he put his face in his hands and thought. A couple of women who formed the only choir chanted their *Gloria in Excelsis*, and he thought, 'If he got as far as this, why isn't he here by now? It took me a few hours across the hills and an hour in the valley: If he got as far as this...' and the knife in his pocket hopelessly answered, 'He was here and he ended here.'

He realised suddenly that all those around him were on their feet and he alone was kneeling. There were no seats and there was a continual coming and going in the mouth of the grotto; the old woman who had been standing next to him when he first came had moved away; an old man succeeded her, a woman... He stood up and heard the priest reciting the Credo: 'I believe, I believe...' and his mind answered firmly, 'Yes, I believe, I believe in the Geiger counters that at this moment men are carrying over the hills, searching for the new veins of uranium; I believe in the mines at Eisleben, the concentration points beyond Halle.' '*Et in unum Dominum*

Jesum Christum.' 'I believe in the crushing mills, the daily input and output, the railway trucks moving east.' 'Who for us men and our salvation.' 'I believe that somewhere here he died to save the world. Do these old women think they can save it this way?' '*Descendit de caelis.*'

A voice in English said, 'Kneel, kneel quickly,' and he saw that all around him the people were on their knees. When he rose again he looked at the woman beside him, but as he said later he knew at once without seeing her who had spoken. He was so certain that this voice could belong only to that face, he was in no hurry to prove his guess true. As he knelt he looked everywhere but at her and for the first time noticed the hard observant gaze of a man who knelt round the edge of the altar, so that three quarters of the congregation was in his view. A shaven head, fat neck, absurd green shorts. Men of the same profession have a knack of recognising each other; a murderer knows a detective because after all he belongs to the same profession, though to a different branch. Brown was not a murderer but nor was this man a detective – like Brown he belonged to the underground, he was stamped with the seal of a police agent, even in the silly green shorts.

It was only then, when he rose, that he bothered to confirm his belief. One look was all he allowed himself: there would never in life, he thought then, be time to look enough; one had to deal with the world and the world was the police agent, the necessity to stay alive. For a moment he tried to catch her gaze, but she looked only at the altar – it was as if she had put in his hand the only help she could. Presently with others she went to the altar rails to take her Communion. Suddenly there were no kneeling figures any more between the police agent and himself – while the priest moved round the rail of the altar they looked at each other across the cave mouth. This was something Brown could understand. If only, he thought, it was a gun I had in my pocket instead of two holy medals: the world is controlled by uranium, not by God. He rose slowly to his feet and, turning his back on the altar, moved away: there was nothing wrong in moving; people came and went all the time. It was only when he was twenty yards away he remembered, 'I should have genuflected.' The desire to look behind him was almost irresistible.

As he walked down the hill past the women moving up he prepared himself in advance for an interrogation. He took the photograph out of his wallet and chewed it until it was a meaningless pulp that he spat out beside the path. Lies too easily give out; one must be ready, as far as possible, with the truth. I am Richard Brown, an English writer, I am writing a book about the Harz, its people, its superstitions. I came over here from Bad Harzburg to see this place of pilgrimage. I know I have no business to be here. I know you have every right to arrest me and investigate me, but that's the truth, the sole truth, will you please get in touch with the British resident at Goslar? After he had gone a hundred yards, he looked round: high up the track a small figure with fat exposed knees came trotting down, past the Stations of the Cross. The end already?

If one is to keep one's nerve, one must not run away. Brown sat down under a fir tree by the path and taking out his knife prepared to cut himself a piece of bread. The figure came slowly on down the hill, a very bourgeois figure now that it had placed a respectable green Homburg hat with a kind of shaving brush in it over the pink head. It never occurred to Brown that he might be mistaken: that wide flat pasty Teutonic face, blank and anonymous, reminded him of a prison wall. You would have had to excavate to find the eyes. Brown opened his knife and cut himself a slice. The man stopped a few yards away and looked at him. '*Guten Morgen*,' Brown said, and to save speaking further words put the bread into his mouth. The man said nothing, watching him eat. Suddenly Brown thought: why did she speak to me in English? What is so English about me? The man's silence disconcerted him. It was as though somewhere poking out of his pocket he carried his country's flag. He cut himself another slice of bread and to conceal his uneasiness he began to play with the knife. So many times when he was a boy he had opened that crooked blade, which he was always told was used for taking stones from horses' hoofs; the only use he had ever made of it was to dig up tough weeds in the garden at Shepperton.

The man in the Homburg turned momentarily away from him and raised his hand. On the road at the foot of the hill two policemen jumped off their bicycles. 'So I don't see the curtain rise,' Brown thought, tugging at the stiff blade and reciting in his own mind that nearly true story: 'I am Richard Brown, an English writer. I am writing a book about the Harz.' The policemen were climbing the hill; they had unslung their rifles. Two old people muttering their prayers before the Station of the Cross did not even look up at them. Well, if we were fighting for survival there was this to be said for the old people; they had survived a long time, longer than he was likely to do.

The tool opened. It had become stuck because wedged in the fork was a tiny scrap of paper on which numerals were written. So that the man in the Homburg should not see what he was doing, Brown rose to his feet and began to walk down the hill. As he walked he made a bread pellet and screwed the paper inside it. Then, with the motion of a man who is troubled by wax, he pushed the pellet into his ear. It occurred to him that if they beat him about the head the pellet would probably fall out, but it was the best he could do under the circumstances.

The policemen stopped and waited for him – or was it only, a wild hope struck him, for the man in the Homburg? Were his nerves inventing a danger that wasn't there? Would they let him pass? '*Guten Morgen*,' he said to the policemen and all his hopes died when the man behind him spoke quietly in English, 'Perhaps you would not mind coming with us to the police station?'

Chapter three

On the desk when he turned round from the wall he could see the contents of his pockets spread out – the knife was there, his cigarette case, his passport, his money – East German marks and *BAF*s – two holy medals, a novel of Turgenev's that he had not quite had time to finish, and a candle he had forgotten to light. Then his knees gave way, and the clock that had been at eye level soared up out of sight towards the ceiling. He saw only the well-polished boots of the two policemen and the fat knees of the man in the Homburg hat. He said, 'My name is Richard Harz. I was an English author. I am writing a book about the… I mean my name is Richard Brown.'

'You have told us all that,' the man in the Homburg said. 'Now you have rested, Mr Brown, please stand up again facing the wall. No, as before please, you may support yourself with your fingers – no, the same two fingers, Mr Brown.'

They were like little shapeless lumps of red putty but they had not lost the feeling of flesh.

'I am telling them to send out for some beer and cigarettes, Mr Brown. Soon you will like to sit down and relax and have a good drink. What made you cross into this zone, Mr Brown?'

'Superstitions of the Harz.'

'What is your rank?'

'English author.'

'To what organisation do you belong?'

'Writing a book.'

The door opened and closed behind him. He prayed to somebody he didn't believe in: don't let them pour the beer into the glass so that I can hear. A clock struck five and he thought: six hours. In the War they had always been given a time limit before a mission – after so many hours you can tell everything, but on this occasion he was quite alone – there was no limit, just as there was no war. He longed for someone to strike him – that would be the beginning of the end.

'For whom are you writing your report?'

With a dying humour he said, 'William Heinemann.'[11]

'How do you spell the name? Is he a West German?' There was an eager note in the Homburg's voice.

Another voice that he had not heard before said, 'Mr Brown is joking, it is the name of an English publisher, see – the name is on this book. Come and sit down, Mr Brown.'

He turned; he wondered whether the worst was about to begin. The newcomer was in a green uniform with officer's badges, a man of much his own age and much his own build. From his face you might have said, of much the same experience.

'Captain Starhov,' he announced.

'Starhov,' Brown said, 'Starhov.'

He sat heavily down and winced when his two fingers touched the desk. 'Starhov,' he said. 'There was a character… which book?…'

'A comic character, Mr Brown. An elderly libertine. Do you read Russian?'

'No. There is a good translation…'

'No translations can convey the style…'

Brown suddenly began to laugh. He put his head in his hands and laughed. When he looked up the Russian was watching him with sad unsmiling patience. 'I am sorry,' Brown said, 'it sounded like a conversation at home. We should go on to agree that poetry is really untranslatable.'

'I know very little about poetry,' the Russian said.

He said to the Homburg hat, 'Pour Mr Brown a drink.'

'And suddenly,' Brown told my informant, 'I began to cry. I don't know why except that always when you are tired, any kindness... I knew this was the most dangerous moment of all up till now. I was capable of sobbing out the truth; I wanted desperately to ask him one question. I had such a strong conviction that he would tell me the truth. And then suddenly before I had time to recover he asked me exactly that.'

'Have you ever heard of a man calling himself Kramer, Paul Kramer?' Captain Starhov asked.

Brown shut his eyes to try to hold the tears in.

'Kramer? Paul Kramer?'

'No,' Brown said. 'No, I've never heard of him.'

'A younger man than you, with a scar running from the left eye?...'

Brown shook his head.

'He too was interested in this grotto of ours.'

'I tell you,' Brown said savagely, 'I don't know the man.'

'Drink your beer, Mr Brown, these fools had no business to question you the way they did.'

The glass of beer stood there like a temptation. It is foolish to resist a temptation too long. Brown drank.

'You are not a Catholic, Mr Brown?'

'No.'

'Why did you buy these holy medals?'

'I have two children who are.'

'Your wife is a Catholic?'

'She's dead.'

'I'm sorry, Mr Brown.'

'It's no concern of yours.'

The sad tempting eyes watched him. 'Of course you think this is part of my performance. You are wrong. One may know what it is to lose someone one loves – or to fear…'

Captain Starhov never moved his eyes. 'I know also that one can use one's own experience quite cold-bloodedly to trap another person. You are right to distrust me as I am right to distrust you.'

'You speak English very well.'

'We have good schools in Russia, whatever your propaganda may say.'

'Are you going to release me?'

'Of course, in time. But you must expect us to check your story.'

'Will that take long?'

'So much depends, Mr Brown.'

'Where will you keep me?'

Captain Starhov spoke sharply in German to the man in the Homburg, but Brown missed what was said. He felt hopelessly tired, beaten… Captain Starhov said, 'They have only two cells in the station here.'

'I am not a criminal.'

'I could take you to my house, but it is not a very easy house to guard. I would have to ask for your parole.'

What an odd old-fashioned word it sounded, Brown thought. I must not show myself too eager.

He said, 'I will give it to you for a week.'

* * *

They drove into what seemed in the dusk a vast courtyard. An eighteenth-century stone house faced a long line of stables: one side of the great square was formed by the houses of the workers – a whole village seemed to be enclosed there. Even a church stood like a mere barn in a corner of the courtyard, part of the farm. The farm carts were driving in – long low vans with two horses apiece, beating up the dust like chaff. Captain Starhov said, 'The house will be pulled down, of course, in the end. The farm has been collectivised.'

'Who lived here?'

'The owner. I have let the owner stay for the time being. It is convenient as long as I am here.'

A soldier opened the door of the car and Captain Starhov stood for a moment, watching the low shadows of the buildings: a horse whinnied in the stables, and the carts drove slowly in. He said, 'I have read of such places in books, but never before...'

'Do you expect to go?'

'We always move on,' Starhov said gloomily.

'It's very beautiful here.'

Starhov turned his back abruptly on the courtyard and led the way into the house. The hall was almost bare: an old stove, a wooden chair, and the eighteenth-century curved staircase had lost part of its balustrade. Grandeur had died a long while ago. Starhov said, 'The soldier will show you your room. You will want to rest. At dinner we can talk again.' As Brown turned away, he added, with a note of surliness, 'Will you leave me your book until then?'

Brown said, 'They have already examined it for marks at the police station.'

Starhov said stiffly, 'If you would do me the favour...'

The room was almost as bare as the hall and almost as large; a narrow iron bedstead, a stove that didn't work, a wash-hand stand, one chair and one light in the centre of the ceiling. It was better than a cell and easier to escape from. As soon as he was alone he took the pellet of bread from his ear. He disinterred the scrap of paper, but the writing was so small he had to climb on the chair and hold it nearer the light to read the little rows of figures which only he could decipher – as soon as he could safely work out his square. He memorised them and then, because they had removed his matches, he screwed the paper back into the bread pellet and swallowed both. There had been one chance in a thousand that he would find the knife, that the message would ever be read; life certainly at times taught one to hope for the impossible. After all, even now he might be of use.

He looked out of the window; the dark was nearly here. He had memorised the direction they had taken from Ilsenhof as well as he was able. As for his parole, that might be of importance to a soldier to whom sanctions applied, but he was no soldier. When once he had deciphered the message he would decide how to act. From the stables a woman crossed the great shadowy square. It was so nearly dark that he could not believe the evidence of his eyes.

He left his room and, waiting on the balcony of the hall, he watched the handle move. Once he had seen her, twice, and now the third time she came into his life and looked up at him, this time not as a stranger but as a face he had remembered all through the hours of interrogation, and he grinned stupidly back at her because in that moment he was happy. He didn't care that there was no welcome, only resentment in her look. To feel oneself, however momentarily, part of a design is like peace. It was the nearest he had ever come to belief. He was relieved of responsibility. He was in the hands of a god.

She said, 'Who are you?' not moving from the door.

'Richard Brown,' he said.

'I don't know you.'

'I have seen you twice before – you came into a shop to buy bread.'

'Does Nicolai?…'

'Captain Starhov has invited me to stay. You see, there wasn't enough room at the police station.'

'You'd have been better off there.'

'I doubt it,' he said, and held out his raw and swollen fingers.

She flinched and looked quickly away. 'I'll try and find some oil if you'll let me by.'

'Let you by? But I am up here and you are down there. I'm not blocking the stairs.'

She said with bewilderment, 'Of course, I don't know what I meant. It was a foolish thing to say.'

She walked quickly to the stairs and climbed them with head bent. She said, 'I'll send somebody with bandages to your room,' moving away from him.

He said, 'I don't want to let you by,' and she stopped and looked back at him.

'What do you mean?'

He said slowly, as though he were reciting a mathematical equation, 'Any passage, any path, any doorway you have to pass, I'd like to be there blocking the way.'

She replied immediately with an honesty that confused him as though she were announcing the second half of the equation, 'You *have* been – all today.' She went on with what seemed to be anger. 'You won't be satisfied till I say it, will you? Alright, I have said it. I have spoken two words to you today. This morning. And now I have said that to you. You have got your triumph. Now for God's sake let me alone.'

'But why? I don't understand.'

'It can happen to a woman, can't it, just as much as to a man? You stood there like a fool while we knelt.'

'Three words, not two, "kneel", you said, "kneel quickly".'

'I didn't see you go away. I was praying – praying that I'd never see you again because you'd be safe.'

'I'm glad I don't believe in prayer…'

'Is Nicolai here?'

'Do you mean Starhov? Yes.'

'He can probably hear every word we are saying.'

'Does it matter?'

'Yes, I love him.'

It was like a douche of cold water in the face.

'And me?' he asked wearily. 'I am sorry. I'm tired. Confused. I didn't understand. I thought you said…'

'It's an obsession. We can get rid of an obsession, can't we? In one way or another. I'll come to your room if you want me to when Nicolai is asleep.' She opened the door and there Starhov was asleep at his desk with a book open before him. It occurred as a new fact to Brown that Russians too were human.

* * *

Starhov stirred his coffee. He said, 'I am a reasonable man like you. I had a good scientific education at Stalingrad. I have no sympathy at all with these superstitious pilgrims, but to suppress them at the present moment would do more harm than good. The General at Erfurt had given orders to destroy the grotto. I countermanded them.'

'Countermanded a general's orders, Captain Starhov?'

'A captain in the MKVD[12] does not take instructions from a general. I told him there were two reasons why the pilgrimages should continue. It is good propaganda in the West and it keeps the people contented. This is not a Catholic population but pilgrims have always come from Czechoslovakia. He was anxious about the security at Eisleben.'

'Eisleben?'

He realised at once that he had made a mistake: he realised too that his interrogation had not finished: at the police station it had only begun. Clara watched him with anxiety.

'Mr Brown, surely you won't pretend that you know nothing of the uranium mines at Eisleben? It has been in the papers. There is no secret. Why do you pretend?'

'Of course I know about the uranium, but Eisleben – I'd forgotten the name.'

'I suppose it is a more important name to us. I took a big risk when I countermanded the General's orders. If anything should go wrong, it will be my responsibility. I have to watch my step very carefully. My orderly reports on me. My second in command would like me to go. The military... In my position one trusts nobody. Nobody at all.' Was it a coincidence, Brown wondered, that he looked across the table at Clara?

'Give Mr Brown another cup of coffee.'

As Brown took the cup from Clara, Starhov said, 'A week ago we caught an agent here.'

Brown saw that Starhov was not watching his face but his hand that held the coffee cup. He stiffened the muscles of his hand to resist, but he heard the cup chink in its saucer. He tried rapidly to cover himself. He said with much irritation, 'I wish you'd drop this idea that I am a spy. It's too melodramatic. Surely spies are little men on salary who watch railway crossings and steal blotting paper... or so I have read.' He worked himself up into irritation to explain the shaking of his hands. 'Did you find any markings in my book?'

Starhov said, 'A book code does not require marks. Do you really read Turgenev, Mr Brown?'

'Yes...'

'Do you remember Insarov?'

'The Bulgarian whose country was oppressed by foreigners?'

'Yes... And Harlov?'

'*The Lear of the Steppes.*'

'Yes.'

'And do you remember, Captain Starhov, *A Month in the Country?*'

He had passed that examination.

'Always the early autumn,' Starhov said, 'and love just beginning – not ending, petering out, no quarrelling except as young people quarrel. Summer lightning. Sometimes it rains even in Turgenev. And the puddles are full of autumn leaves.'

'It was a very different Russia.'

'You have to lose something,' Starhov said, 'when you make something. A carpenter's floor is covered with sawdust, isn't it, scraps of wood.' He said moodily, 'I wasn't only looking for marks in your book, Mr Brown. That was my first purpose. But afterwards I fell asleep reading. It was odd reading Turgenev in English. Passages I knew by heart in Russian came to me as though they were by a strange writer. There is one that goes…' And Starhov began to speak in Russian – a few sentences only.

'I would like to learn Russian,' Brown said. 'For the sake of Turgenev. Not for Dostoevsky, not even Tolstoy. They are too great and important and stormy.'

'Read me that passage in English, Mr Brown.'

'You would have to find it for me.'

'Of course, I forgot. One always thinks other people speak one's own language.'

But had he thought that, Brown wondered, or had he laid another inconspicuous trap, had he some reason to suppose that indeed he did know Russian?

Lights passed across the great farmyard: a soldier with an electric torch, a woman carrying a lighted ember. In the stable a stallion neighed and kicked his stall. Clara rose to draw the curtains.

'Let them be,' Starhov said, 'there is nothing to conceal here, not at this moment. Three people together in a quiet house in the country, and one reading a book. In a house like this, that must have been a common sight. Before the War, before your husband was killed, it must have happened many times, Clara.'

'I suppose so. I wouldn't remember a thing like that.'

'And yet it has never happened before to me. Here is the passage, Mr Brown.'

Brown read: 'It was an exquisite day; I fancy there are no days like that in September anywhere but in Russia. The stillness was such that one could hear, a hundred paces off, the squirrel hopping over the dry leaves, and the broken twig just feebly catching at the other branches and falling at last on the soft grass – to lie there for ever, not to stir again till it rotted away. The air, neither warm nor chill but only fragrant, and as it were keen, was faintly, deliciously stinging in my eyes and on my cheeks.'[13]

Brown looked across at Starhov. He sat with bent head, and his index finger, his trigger finger twitched and twitched on his knee. Brown read on: 'A long spider web, delicate as a silver thread, with a white ball in the middle, floated smoothly in the air and sticking to the butt-end of my gun, stretched straight out in the air – a sign of settled and warm weather. The sun shone with a brightness as soft as moonlight.'

'Thank you, Mr Brown.' He repeated the last phrase in Russian. He lifted his hand from his knee. 'This week two men have been shot. I had to give the *coup de grâce* myself.' Again he looked quickly up at Brown: it was almost as though he were imploring him to put an end to all this quiet together in the lamplit room with the big yard all around them and the gentle movements in the stove, to make life normal again. The agent. The informer. The long interrogation. The ordinary understandable world. Confess, he seemed to implore, but the only confession was his own. '"The sun shone with a brightness as soft as moonlight," that's Russian too.'

Brown lay awake listening for a sound he did not expect and when at last at two in the morning it came, he felt disappointment. When you are in love only then all the pains and longings are small, almost pleasurable like sensation coming back to a dead limb, but after possession too often one loves, and love is hard and cruel and jealous, love is selfish. 'I want, I want' becomes the burden in the mind. But when she was quiet again by his side, there was no room between their bodies for regret, there was only joy and peace. He felt for that moment that he would never be in love again. They didn't even speak until she said, 'I have to go. If I fall asleep now, I feel I shall never wake up again.'

'The obsession – have you got rid of it?'

'No. Now you have driven it in too deep.'

Chapter four

He had trained his memory so well that it never occurred to him that he could forget a short cipher, but the next morning he struggled in vain with that last message. The only word that emerged from the mutilations was 'wax' and that might itself be a mutilation. He thought, 'What a failure I am.' There was nothing to do now but get back across the border and report the loss of a better agent than himself.

A soldier brought him coffee in his room and later in the morning he saw Starhov drive out of the courtyard. He felt an odd relationship with him, a kindliness, because they loved the same woman. For the first time he regretted the need to break his parole. It might very well mean death to Starhov. And all for the sake of a meaningless word – 'wax.'

He had left the door open, so that he could see Clara go by and he called to her immediately she passed. She came and stood in the doorway and he thought, 'I have never loved a beautiful woman before.' It worried him. He felt hopelessly insecure because the whole world must want her.

'Yes?'

'Come in,' and it astonished him that she obeyed him.

'Close the door.' He thought, 'If there was a mirror I would look at myself, I must be different to what I thought I was – I must be worthwhile.' He said, 'Starhov's gone, I saw him go.' He turned her towards the window and put his hands on her breasts and the back of her head was against his neck and he could feel on his body the division of her thighs, like an impress on sand.

'There'll be tonight,' she said.

'One never knows.'

'His orderly is in the next room.'

'Lock the door.'

'There's no key.' Suddenly she took his hands off her and walked over to the bed. 'It doesn't matter,' she said, 'it doesn't matter.'

When they were quiet again, for the first time they talked. He had the sense that life would not be long enough to contain all the talking they had to do.

'How old are you?' he asked.

'Thirty. You?'

'Forty-eight. A big difference.'

'Not so great. When I am forty-five you will be only sixty-three. It's a good age, sixty-three. Are you a writer or is that a story?'

'I have written a few books. Why were you at the grotto?'

'It was Sunday. It's the only place left for mass.'

'Was it? I didn't know. Are you a Catholic then?'

'Yes.'

'And you believe all that – the vision – the rose?'

'I think it may be true. Why were you there?'

'They asked me that at the police station for six hours. I told them I was writing a book about the Harz Mountains and its superstitions.'

'Are you?'

'No.'

'What are you doing?'

He looked at her. It was the stock situation of all melodramas; you were trapped by a woman. But was it possible to love and not to trust – most of the time, in most things? He said cautiously, 'I was looking for somebody.'

'A man called Kramer?'

A man was whistling his way across the yard. He remembered three people in a room reading a book. Why couldn't the world be like that?

'Yes,' he said.

'Who was he?'

'My brother – my half-brother.'

She began to cry. He said, 'My dear, my dear, I've guessed he's dead. I knew it really before I came over here. These things happen.'

'Did you love him?'

'Yes.' She turned her head on the pillow as though she could stop tears as you stop blood, with the pressure of a bandage. He said, 'We had the same mother. She left my father. I don't blame her. She loved somebody else. It happens, doesn't it? I didn't meet my brother until five years ago. She married a German, you see. He was very like her except for his scar.'

She whispered something he could not hear.

'Yes?'

'Your mother?'

'Oh,' he said with false lightness, 'we killed her. For all I know I killed her myself. You see, I was in the RAF.'

'And I killed your brother.'

He tried to brush it aside, 'Oh, the Russians did that. Or the East Germans.'

'No,' she said, 'I mean it. I killed him myself.'

'What's troubling you?' he asked and tried to touch her hair, but she moved her head away and lay with her back to him.

'I killed him,' she said, 'I gave him away. I saw him there in the grotto just as I saw you. He wasn't a Catholic either and he made the same mistakes. Afterwards I sent a message to Nicolai and I followed him. He had gone into a shop that sells – oh statues and things. They arrested him there. He was turning over a tray of medals. I don't know why.'

He said bitterly, 'And then they stood him against a wall propped on two fingers for hours on end. Why did you do it? You aren't a Russian.'

'I love Nicolai,' she said. 'Where would I be if it wasn't for him? Without a home. In a labour camp. Then I saw that man. I thought this is the end of Nicolai. He allowed the pilgrimages. He guaranteed the security. He protected us.'

'For the sake of propaganda.'

'How do you know? How do I know? He is a man. He can do stupid things for love, like the rest of us.'

She got off the bed and made for the door keeping her face away from him. She said, 'We should never have talked. Just made love till we got tired of it. Not talked.'

As she felt for the handle he asked, 'Why did you tell me to kneel? Why didn't you send for Nicolai again?'

She answered him bitterly between the opening and the closing of the door, 'Because I fell in love. At first sight. Like a schoolgirl.'

When she had gone, he looked at his two fingers. 'Paul,' he said, 'Paul.' Then furiously he began to tear at the cool comforting white bandages that soothed his hurt.

* * *

Starhov said, 'So far the reports are favourable. You seem undoubtedly to be Mr Brown who writes books. The British resident at Goslar is making inquiries. He has asked for our assistance.'

Brown lit a cigarette. 'What did you reply?'

'That we had no trace of you at present, but that we were making inquiries. Where is Clara?'

'I haven't seen her since this morning.'

Starhov got restlessly up. 'She is nearly always here when I come back from town. Perhaps she is about the farm. They do not like her there because of me.' He led the way out of the house and across the courtyard. He said, 'I gave them everything and yet they hate her because she gave me – a little.'

They searched for her in vain, in the stables, the dairy. Men spoke to Starhov subserviently, and he barked out his questions at them like an owner. Brown said, 'What will happen to her when you move on?' and got no reply. He said, rubbing the sore spot in his mind, 'She is very fond of you.'

'I cannot tell that,' Starhov said. The twilight was coming down: it was the hour for intimacies that later one regrets. He said, 'I had read about women like her. I had never met one. Now I still feel as though I had – read about her.' He added with longing, 'If only I had no protection to give her.'

'I don't understand.'

'She needs us all too much. How can we feel trust? Perhaps she loves me. Perhaps she loves her house. There are so many refugees anywhere needing foodcards, needing passports. How does a man learn to trust when he has authority?'

'And yet you trusted my parole?'

Starhov grinned at him with unhappy humour. 'I expected you to break it last night. You wouldn't have got two miles from here. Every path is guarded.' He added, 'It was a point in your favour that you did not try.'

Brown thought: this man is to be pitied. This man who killed my brother. He said, 'I think you are wrong about her.'

'I was twelve years old when the revolution came. We have watched over and over again how people are trusted – engineers, writers, generals – we have seen them betray us. The men who taught us everything when we were young. Our heroes. They betrayed us.'

They came into the great barn and there they found her lying in the straw, asleep, with an appearance of complete exhaustion. Starhov stood and watched her. He said, 'You see I cannot even trust myself. If she said to me, come across over there, live with me for ever…'

'Would you do it?'

'No. Perhaps a year ago… But people do not live together for ever. There is no such thing as 'For ever.' And yet you can want what you read in books, even though you know that it's always only propaganda, propaganda.'

'Even Turgenev?' Brown asked with malice.

'He makes us want the past, doesn't he? They don't exist any longer in my world or yours, the women of Turgenev.'

As they watched her she woke. She woke with an expression of happiness that immediately faded. She said, 'I have slept a long time. It's nearly dark.'

'You were dreaming,' Brown said.

'Yes.'

'You are beautiful asleep,' Starhov said sadly and Brown turned away thinking of the daily joy of waking and seeing her as she had been then, and he thought angrily how quickly when I watch her I can forget my brother.

That night it was a little past midnight when she came to him. They had dined almost in silence. Even the hidden interrogation had stopped. She said, 'I am not going to stay. Only a moment. Even if you won't speak to me. But this morning I had no time, I was shocked. I had no chance. I wanted to defend myself, but I don't know how.'

He touched her face and said with a kind of despair, 'This is your defence.'

'I wanted you to know – he didn't suffer. He was shot at once trying to escape.'

'I wonder if my mother suffered. My dear, my dear,' he said, 'we all have so much guilt it cancels out.'

'I wanted – before you went home… You'll be going home soon?'

'If he doesn't find out…'

'Is there so much to find out? No, don't tell me.'

'You had no reason to tell me what you had done. You could have kept quiet. I may as well be honest too. If we don't trust each other any more than *they* do, it's a bad world.'

'Please tell me nothing, nothing.'

'Paul was bringing back a report – on the Czech mines and the mines at Eisleben. The daily input and output. The number of trucks going eastwards. The position of the laboratories, perhaps even the destination in Russia. He was a good agent. That's why I sent him.'

'You sent him?'

'He was my best agent.'

'They will kill you if they find out.'

'Yes.'

'Then why did you tell me? I can betray you to Nicolai. I can talk in my sleep like other people. I can make a mistake, can't I?'

'It wouldn't matter to me much,' he said. 'I have nothing – not even the report.'

'And if you had got your precious report? – would it have made any difference?'

'The authorities would have had something to put on their card indexes. They might be able – I don't know – to calculate the chances of war next year, the year after...'

'Is that useful?'

He shrugged his shoulders. 'Not very. We'll all be dead anyway then. But this is a profession like any other. We give the best answers we can – the questions may be futile. That's not our responsibility.'

'What are you going to do?'

'I thought I would simply break my parole, but he is not as careless as all that. The place is guarded as well as it can be. And there is no hurry now.'

'But every day you are here, they are investigating...' She said, 'If only you had something to report, you would go. You'd escape somehow. Then it would be your damned duty to save your life.'

'Paul left a message, but I can only work out one word. He was ciphering against time perhaps.'

'What word?'

' "Wax". If he guessed he was followed – he must have guessed that, then he would have tried to hide the report and have left some clue.'

She said, 'He knelt when other people stood, and stood when they knelt. He crossed himself wrong, like you. He went up and took Communion – I hated him for that.'

He asked with wonder, 'You really do believe?'

'Yes.'

'You pray at night? You really think that God answers prayers?'

'Yes.'

'And still wars come. And the atom bomb goes off.'

'We don't all pray for what matters.'

'Don't we pray for peace in all the churches?'

'And what sort of peace do we mean – the Council of Europe, the powers of UNO? They are toys, aren't they? And twenty years ago we prayed for the League of Nations.'

'What do you pray for?'

'Oh, I pray for stupid things, contradictory things – that Nicolai will somehow survive. That you will be alive next week. Sometimes I remember to pray that I shall love God. If we loved God do you think all this would exist?'

He said, 'I can't get further than loving a woman.'

'My dear,' she said, 'my dear. Some people can't even do that. Nicolai…'

'Doesn't he love you?'

'He doesn't believe in me. He doesn't trust me. I gave him your brother's life, but he doesn't trust me.'

'You can give him mine now.'

She said sadly, 'No. I am going to give you his. You are going to have everything – even your precious report.'

'I'd almost forgotten the report.'

'When your brother knelt, after he had seen his mistake, there was a bracket for candles. Candles are made of wax aren't they?'

'I don't understand.'

'There is always a deposit of old candle wax in the socket. If the report was small enough…'

'He would have used microfilm.'

'He could have gouged out a hole for it and lit another candle on top. And I don't suppose anyone ever clears the wax away.'

'Can I get to the grotto?'

'We can try. You couldn't get away yourself, but I think I know where Nicolai stations his men.' She added with bitterness, 'Two children thought they saw the Mother of God and she gave them a rose. Candles have always burnt there ever since and now under one of them is a spy's report on the output of uranium.'

'I'm sorry,' he said.

'And so is she. But she's sorry for the whole world, not for Western Union.'

* * *

They met again on the balcony at the head of the stairs.

'Asleep?'

She whispered back, 'He sleeps like the dead always. Poor Nicolai.'

He started to go down, but she put her hand on his arm. 'Wait. He has a sentry at the front of the house. You can see his shadow when he passes the window.'

'And I really believed him when he asked for my parole.'

'There,' she said. 'Now count until he returns.'

After a while the shadow came back.

'Now again the other way.'

It took the sentry three minutes to the left and then three and a half minutes to the right. 'When he next goes to the right, we have one and three-quarter minutes to get clear.'

Brown said, 'Are the grounds lighted?'

'No. Aim a little to the left, the corner of the stables.'

They went down the hall and stood with the backs of their hands touching by the cold stove. She shivered.

'You should have brought a coat.'

'No,' she said, 'if we don't get clear it's not so incriminating…'

The shadow passed going to the left. She said, 'You can buy me a coat – in England.' It was the first time she had admitted in so many words that she was going with him – the whole way. Suddenly he felt fear. She so belonged to this place, he couldn't conceive it possible that a time would come when they could wake daily in a peaceful world – peaceful until the bomb fell.

He said, 'I have two children...'

'I would like you to have a third.'

The shadow passed going to the right. He said, 'Pray. I can't...' She opened the door and led the way onto the steps, and suddenly she was lit up. She stood braced and still against the blinding light. Her whisper hardly reached him, 'Get back upstairs. Into your room,' and as he went the sound of a car driving in through the gates of the farm reached him; she scrambled on the path as the sentry came back. He thought, thank God we were not half across the yard, that she was not wearing her coat.

At the window of his room he looked straight down on the car. A stout man wearing a green Homburg hat held the door for the General to descend; the shaving brush in his hat pointed like a pistol upwards to Brown's face. He heard Clara's voice saying in German, 'A late hour, General,' and as the General entered the house the man looked up, the sunken eyes seemed to screw up in an attempt to penetrate the darkness between them, and in his two fingers Brown felt the nerve of pain beating again.

Through his open door he heard Starhov going downstairs. A harsh angry voice could be heard at intervals; he could not hear Starhov's answers: then the voice moved out of hearing and a few minutes later an orderly summoned him below.

Both men were on their feet, Starhov in his dressing gown, the General booted and medalled, a younger man than Starhov with a blunted Mongol face. Starhov said, 'The General wanted to take a look at you. You are dressed?'

'I could not sleep,' Brown said. 'I was going to take a walk in the yard.'

'You had better tell me first another time so that the sentry can be warned.'

The General asked angrily in Russian what they were discussing and Starhov replied curtly that they were talking of insomnia. Brown's Russian was not adequate to understand the argument that boomed and growled like a storm over his head. Starhov turned suddenly and said, 'You can go now. I must apologise for the stupidity of this man.' For a moment he thought the General would bar the way, but he contented himself with spitting on Starhov's polished floor.

Clara stood on the balcony above the hall. He looked up at her and said, 'We were lucky,' then turned and saw where the man in the Homburg stood quietly watching them from beside the stove.

* * *

Starhov said, 'It's quiet now that he has gone.' He had come to Brown's room and lay back on Brown's bed with an effect of intimacy, assumed or not, Brown was uncertain.

'What did he want?'

'He had only just heard of your presence. He thought I should have told him and that you should have been kept at the police station. He also considered I was wrong in interrupting your interrogation. I told him it had not been interrupted but had been continued in another form. He warned me again about the pilgrimage. I told him he needn't worry. It is my responsibility just as you are.'

'Can a captain talk like that to a general?'

'Generals are two a penny. An MKVD officer does not take orders from a general.'

'And if you are mistaken about me?'

'He will have a chance of revenge.' He turned his head sideways on Brown's pillow and looked at the book beside the bed. 'Not finished the story yet?'

'I have begun it again.'

'If I stayed in one place for a year, perhaps I would have some books too.' His eyes were heavy with sleep.

'Do you in the West ever feel trust?'

'Sometimes.'

'Insarov trusted Bersenyev. He trusted Elena. A strange dead world where men were friends and women were faithful. Where's Clara?'

'She went to her room.'

'That man disturbed me.' He shut his eyes. 'Do you remember who it was in Turgenev who said, "one wants to do nothing, one wants to see no one, one looks forward to nothing, one is too lazy for thought"?...'[14]

'No.'

'Nor do I. But the words stick. In that world they had happy memories, sad memories, not memories that disgust. Sometimes I think we've killed enough men.'

'Starhov, I want to walk for a little in the yard.'

'Yes.'

'I will be coming back.'

'I trust you, why? Trust. That's an odd thing to say. I have fallen in trust.' He lay with his eyes shut. He said, 'The password for the sentries is –' His voice fell so low that Brown had to stoop to catch the word.

'Sleep here for a while. I'll be back in half an hour.'

'Put the book beside me in case I wake,' but before Brown had reached the door Starhov was already asleep – like the dead, like the effigy on his own tomb, Brown thought, except that there would be no effigy on the tomb of one who had committed the crime of trust. Had it been a temptation all his life to which now, at last from mere exhaustion he had succumbed? But why now? why me? because I had read Turgenev? Brown wondered.

* * *

When they were in the comparative security of the forest, she took a gun from her coat pocket and gave it to him. She said, 'It's the first time he ever left it out. Always he locks it up – when it is not at his side or under his pillow.'

'You are wearing your coat.'

'It's too late to bother about evidence now.'

When they were still a quarter of a mile from the grotto they could detect it by the flicker of the candles the pilgrims had lit. They reached the path a hundred yards below the grotto and walked up together past the hideous Stations. There was no point now in concealment. He said, 'We have to reach the boundary before daylight,' but he had no belief that he would ever find himself again in the world of officers' wives and British clubs and of NAAFI shops. He wasn't even certain that he desired them.

'What are you thinking?' she asked.

'I was wondering whether we should end here where we began.' The Mother of God held out her absurd pink rose and he stood while Clara knelt. There was no need any longer to do the right thing. One old woman knelt by a rack of candles telling her rosary. When Clara rose he asked her, 'On which side did Paul?...' She indicated the old woman, and he stood beside her waiting for her to move. Steadily the old woman worked through her beads. The process was endless. He looked at his watch and saw how far the night had advanced. Only one candle that presumably the old woman had lit was burning in the bracket.

Cautiously he scraped at the first candle holder with his finger – there were six of them. He found nothing there. The second had too little wax left in it to conceal anything larger than a pea. The chances were a hundred to one, he thought, that the film – if the report had been filmed – had been found. The woman muttered her prayers. Where had she come from at this hour of the night? Where could she possibly find a lodging? What was the passion that drove these people?

Brown felt a tide of sympathy for Starhov. Uranium against uranium. The mines in the Harz against the mines in the Congo. In a way, they were allies, doing the same job of destruction. He looked at her, but she would not look at him though she knelt at his side – the third, the fourth, the fifth holder contained nothing, there remained only one holder where the candle was burning. The old woman reached the end of her beads and started all over again. Brown put out his hand and snatched the candle and the flame flickered and went out. 'No,' Clara said, 'No.' The old woman looked up from her beads. She looked at him with astonishment and grief. She said in German, 'It is for my son.' He dug his finger into the soft wax, and felt, to his own surprise, the little tight roll. While the woman watched him he put the candle back and felt for a match. He had no match.

'Come away,' he said to Clara, but she had taken the candle and crossed the grotto to re-light it at another flame. He waited with impatience and saw at the entrance to the cave the man with the Homburg hat.

* * *

Brown said, 'He must have followed us all the way through the forest. He had obviously stayed behind when the General left. He had gone over, I suppose, to the General's side, feeling fairly certain that Starhov would lose in the end. Of course, he couldn't have guessed that I would be armed.

'He could not see me very clearly, all the light was on the other side of the grotto where Clara was lighting the old woman's candle. It was my duty to shoot and my pleasure to shoot. It was my duty to go back across the border with that roll, and it was my pleasure to revenge the two damaged fingers – and Paul. I suppose it was the damaged finger on the right hand that made my shot miss: it crashed into the grotto wall among the offerings and the tin hearts and legs. I wonder if he would have hung a piece of himself up there if he had survived?

'I called to Clara, "Put out the candles," just as he fired again. His bullet scraped my left hand, so that I dropped the roll and the bullet went on to bury itself in the Virgin's image. I could hear the plaster crack. Then the candles went out and he was standing clearly in the moonlight. He peered and I came cautiously forward. I wasn't going to let my damaged finger interfere this time. I shot again when I was quite certain. The hat rolled a little way down the path.

'I went back into the grotto to find the film and Clara. There was no light to see by, but I found the roll quite soon. I could tell at once from the feel that it was quite useless – the bullet had ripped it into wastepaper. I put it in my pocket as a souvenir of a hopeless mission. Clara was kneeling by the dead man. I said, "There is nothing you can do for him."

'She said, "You are so damned certain of everything, aren't you? I can pray, can't I?" She looked down at that ugly face as though he were her brother.'

I said to Brown, 'And then?'

'That's all,' he said, 'There wasn't any time to lose. The Ilsenhof police would have heard the firing. We made good time to the border, and there a patrol stopped us. I thought it was an

Eastern patrol, so I threw away my gun and what was left of Paul's report. The only one who brought anything away was Clara.'

'What did she bring?'

'Three quarters of a plaster rose.'

I told him, 'That's all that's left of the grotto. The pilgrim passes have been stopped and this time I think the place has really been dynamited. We heard rumours that a new MKVD officer had arrived in the district.'

'Poor Starhov,' Brown said. 'It was bad luck, wasn't it, that he started trusting just when I came on the scene.'

'It's bound to happen sometime.'

'Is it?' Brown said. I couldn't understand his look of misery.

'And Clara?'

'Oh,' he said, 'we are getting married. Of course she will be a British citizen then, with a British passport.'

'Good luck to both of you.'

He looked at his two fingers – they were nearly healed now. He said, 'Redburn, I don't know you from Adam. We've only met two or three times, but,' he broke out, 'there was something Starhov said that I can't get out of my mind. "She needs us all too much, how can we feel trust?",' and it was then that Clara came into my office to find him. I hadn't seen her before and I felt like shaking Brown and telling him what a fool he was. You see, she was not only beautiful, she was perfectly – convincing. I wished that I could stake a lifetime on her.

I saw them again. It was the last night of the week's drama festival and they sat together four rows behind me. The platitudinous judge in the dinner jacket finished his discourse on 'Excellent characterisation' and 'Clever production' and the cup was handed over by the C.I.C. I could hardly believe it, but the prize for acting went to those lifeboat Combers of the first night and one of them came up in his oilskins to receive it. He must have been tipped off or brought them with him on the off chance. We clapped like anything and looking round I saw the future Browns. I gained from that glance no sense of happiness at all and I thought is distrust as infectious as all that? Does it stop at no boundaries?

As we went out, I caught them up. I had what I thought was a last word to say to them. 'Brown,' I said, 'It's been confirmed. Starhov's gone.'

'Where?' he asked rather stupidly.

'We shall never know that.'

Clara turned and walked out of the theatre and stood in the darkness. She didn't want Brown to see her tears. He was in a mood to misunderstand her. I said, 'And that damned grotto...'

'Yes?'

'The thing's happening on our side now. Two labourers instead of two children. The picture dealers and the manufacturers of statues and the photographers are all bothering for concessions and the Russians, of course, would like to issue passes for pilgrims over here.'

'Clara believes in the rubbish,' Brown said, 'or says she does – I wish I did, I wish I believed in anything.' He went on watching Clara where she stood on the steps as the officers went by.

'You are very lucky,' I said. I suppose there was too much warmth in my voice because he turned and looked at me with suspicion. But in my case he was right not to trust. If I have described Brown's story in detail it's because I've heard it from two people, because I swore that night that one thing in life was worth fighting for – after all in the long run Brown had to discover that you can't love and not trust.

The Stranger's Hand

Part One

Chapter one

The child had an air of taking everything in and giving nothing away. At Rome airport he was led across the tarmac by his aunt, but he seemed to hear nothing of her advice to himself or of the information she produced for the air hostess: he was too busy with his eyes – the hangars had his attention, every plane on the field except his own: that could wait.

'My nephew,' she was saying. 'Yes – that's him on the list. Roger Court. You *will* look after him, won't you? He's never been quite on his own before,' but when she made that statement the child's eyes moved back plane by plane with what looked like contempt, back to the large breasts and the fat legs and the over-responsible mouth: 'How *could* she have known,' he might have been thinking, 'when I'm alone, how often I'm alone?'

His aunt was quite capable of holding up the plane with her garrulity: 'If you'll just see him to the *Europa*,' she said, 'when you get to Venice – it is a good hotel, isn't it? He's no trouble, no trouble at all. I've had him on my hands – goodness, long enough to know that. His father's coming home tonight from Trieste.' And she would undoubtedly have gone on to give a testimonial to her brother too if the air hostess had not managed, with a certain brutality, to interrupt her.

'You'll have to say goodbye now,' she said, as the last of the child's fellow-passengers climbed the companion way.

His aunt said emotionally, 'Oh Roger, my dear, Roger,' and made a grab at him, but he evaded her and, turning solemnly halfway up the companion, he made his dry reply, 'Goodbye, Aunt Rose.'

'In a fortnight, dear…' but she was already addressing a back.

It seemed like a deliberate action to avoid her waving hand when he chose his seat on the opposite side of the plane, even though that entailed the danger of some curious stranger sitting down beside him. A child's privacy is never quite secure: nobody even hesitates to intrude: privacy has to be guarded behind a locked door ('how often have I told you not to turn the key?') or in the centre of a hedge ('we looked for you everywhere'). As soon as the plane was in the air, he opened his small attaché case, not forgetting an automatic glance around him, and pulled from between the folds of his pyjamas the copy of a children's paper – a bright gaudy common paper that he had no business, according to his aunt, to waste his time on. He was a little short-sighted, and held his head bent over the paper, like a scholar, while he read how a cruel smile of triumph crossed the features of Mr Hogan.[1] He didn't trouble to undo his safety belt, though the warning light had long gone out, for Mr Hogan had by this time locked the barn door and, taking out his lighter, was about to set fire to the thatch. Roger Court sighed and looked away. It was the end of *that* instalment and it was most unlikely that anywhere in Italy he would find the succeeding number. His brain must provide the sequel. The author – who was called Captain Peter Day – would have undoubtedly seen a way of escape from that barn, though the door was locked and there were no windows, but authors always contrived happy endings, and even at eight years old one knew that all endings were not happy.

'Have you been in an aeroplane before?' The air hostess had sat down beside him, but she received as icy a reception as his aunt.

'Yes,' he said: at that moment the barn was in flames and Major Ronnie Dunne was struggling in the smoke to find a way out, but it was no friendly author now who watched his struggle, ready to point out a convenient trap door: a realist was in charge.

'Was that your mother you were with?'

'No.'

'Is she in Venice?'

'No.'

'In England?'

'No.'

'She's not dead is she?' The air hostess' voice prepared the sympathetic note, but the savagery of his reply silenced her. 'She doesn't live with us any more.'

'Oh,' she said, 'I see,' but to judge from her bewilderment she was as much too young to see as the child was old enough. He could remember the long absences, the strain of nerves that led to sudden punishments and sudden treats, the arrival of his aunt and the strong words that floated up the stairway to the nursery landing, phrases like 'selfish', 'not even for the child', 'let his father do his share', 'love nobody but yourself' – that last was the most often repeated. It lodged in the child's mind in the very tones it was first uttered in, so that sometimes during the two years in Rome, when his aunt appealed in vain for some sign of love – 'after all I've done' – he expected it again to be repeated, expected it with a sense of guilt, for certainly there was no one he was aware of loving. His father wrote to him regularly once a week (it was not his father's fault that he could obtain no leave from Trieste), and his aunt, regularly, every Saturday afternoon, thought of a treat for him. But we do not love people for what they do for us. Love happens to us; it isn't created.

He said reluctantly, because he couldn't help realising that in her own way she intended well: 'My father's a policeman.'

'I thought he worked in Trieste.'

'He does.'

'Oh.' It was the colloquial English phrase she was most adept in. 'You'll be glad to see him, I expect?' but that sentence he obviously considered required no answer, and she left him alone after that, until their arrival. One sign of approval he did give, when he saw that the bus to take him from the airport was a motor launch: an indrawn sigh of satisfaction.

At the *Europa* he was handed over to the reception clerk, and his feet slid on the long floors that glistened like water. He had been handed a letter from his father and he held it screwed and unopened in his hand while he followed the clerk. He was not deceived by the clerk's patronage that took the whimsical form of behaving to him as though he were an adult. The clerk opened a door on the first floor. 'I hope this will suit you, sir,' and he stepped into an enormous room. It seemed to be all floor and light. The jetty on the Grand Canal outside strained and creaked.

'Major Court asked us for a double room, sir. I think you will be comfortable here.'

'Yes,' the child said. He went to the window and stared across the water to the stone steps and the great dome of Santa Maria. A dirty crowded waterbus pushed its way up the Canal, setting the rank of gondolas outside the hotel bumping on its wave. The clerk lingered a moment: he wasn't certain of himself, confronted with a back more concentrated and self-contained than a millionaire's.

'If you want lunch, sir, I can show you the restaurant.'

'Must I?' the child said.

'But aren't you hungry?'

'No.'

'Major Court won't be arriving till the eight o'clock train. He asked us to look after you.'

The child turned rather as a prisoner might turn towards a warder. 'All right,' he said, and followed the clerk back the opposite way, flowers and his own face flashing at him in the continual mirrors as though he were standing like a diver among the underwater plants. The head waiter, taking over from the clerk, put him at a table by the window, so that he could see the traffic to and fro on the Canal: suitcases were being loaded into a gondola at the hotel jetty, and the manager had come out into the sun to speed a passing guest. The gleam and wetness dazzled the boy's eyes, and he turned away towards the almost empty restaurant (it was too early for visitors). Somebody was wheeling towards him a whole table of *hors d'œuvres*. Passively he allowed his plate to be heaped; he would explain to nobody the nausea in his nerves.

When he took up his fork, he remembered the letter crumpled in his right hand. He was forbidden to read at meals, and the hour of open rebellion would not strike for two years or more, so he laid it by his plate and tried to eat. He managed a few beans, a little potato, but the anchovy burnt his tongue with salt and he gave up. He looked secretively this way and that: he longed to make a run for it to the shelter of his room, but a head waiter blocked the doorway. Then a voice spoke beside him: 'Lonesome?'

Yet another grown-up had assumed the right to intrude, and nothing could possibly daunt this one – certainly not the child's monosyllable. Flushed with her wine at lunch, boisterous with the *bonhomie* of the New World, she adored children and knew all about children. Hadn't she five kids of her own back in Philadelphia? There wasn't a thing anybody could tell her about children – and certainly a child couldn't, and she had discovered all the unimportant details about this one from the head porter before she accosted him.

'Too much oil? I felt like that myself the first week. Couldn't eat more than two courses a meal. And you wouldn't be used to butter. Now don't you fast any longer, but come with us and see the sights. We're catching the five o'clock train, but there's time for a runaround first. You'll have a wonderful appetite for your supper.'

She was at any rate powerful and ruthless enough in her assurance to dredge out of him the longest sentence he had formed since sitting down in the Venice plane. 'I've got to wait here for my father – he's coming here.' Even after two years the words 'my father' lay heavily on his tongue. That was what his aunt always called him – with a slight note of disapproval. Once, in very early days, he had challenged her, 'Has Daddy done something wrong?' and her reply left behind a vague impression that all was not as it should be. 'Your father's a good man. Of course he's done nothing *wrong*,' but once he overheard from the stairs the phrase 'a man ought to be able to keep a woman', which, equated with another of his aunt's expressions, 'we can't afford to keep a dog with meat the price it is', gave him the idea that his father had been unable to afford either his mother or himself. Poverty, like the beggars on the Spanish Steps, was shameful, and soon the formal phrase that seemed to remove him further from his father became usual on his tongue.

'But you don't have to stay till he comes,' the American woman said, and at that moment her husband joined her and the *bonhomie* and the boisterousness were increased by exactly one hundred per cent. The restaurant that had seemed empty was full of the two of them. The boy's eyes moved from the man's round soft unlined face that looked as though it had come straight from the kneading fingers of a masseuse to the astonishing hand-painted silk tie, all reds and exotic flowers and a nymph strangled in the knot.

'You're young Roger Court, aren't you? We're going to give you a runaround.'

It was no good fighting against this fate: he was bundled up and tied like a rucksack and flung across the shoulders by their appalling kindness: they sat over him at Florian's until he had finished every bit of a large chocolate ice cream: they ran him through St Mark's as though they were on a steeplechase, giving nicknames to the bearded Byzantine saints: they got him back to the square in time to see the pigeons fed at two: pushed him into a gondola and out again to sit in the glare of a furnace and watch glass, blown out like balloons: back into another gondola with a glass dog clutched, like his father's letter, in his hand. They had the firm conviction that he was lonely, and they talked and bantered so steadily to keep his spirits up that they never noticed his silence. They bought him half a pound of sugar almonds (he couldn't attract their attention long enough to tell them he didn't like almonds), they hauled him onto the jetty to say goodbye and watch them depart by motor boat for the station, and Mrs Loftheim (that was what he made her name out to be) thrust his own handkerchief into his hand to wave with. For a long time he heard their voices come back over the water as they told each other what a cute kid he was, and silence – when it returned at last – was as resonating as a noise. He turned and went back into the hotel, and climbed the stairs to his room (he was too shy to take the lift) and sat down in a corner of the huge room by one of the beds. The glass dog had lost its tail, snapped cleanly off in Mrs Loftheim's last embrace, but the letter was still there unopened.

It was nearly dark: the late sunlight lay on the Canal like the gilding of an eighteenth-century couch: he turned on the bedside light to read his letter.

Dear Roger (the phrase had the same distance as 'my father': they seemed to be signalling to each other tentatively over the No Man's Land of two years, a waste filled with the wreckage of other lives than their own), *I shall be arriving at Venice by the eight o'clock train from Trieste. I'll come straight to the hotel and we'll have dinner together. It won't hurt you, will it, to stay up late one night? I shall be hungry because there's no food on the train, and we don't eat so much here as you do in Italy. It will be fun to see St Mark's with you and the glass-blowing and have rides in gondolas.*

Have I got to do all that again, the child wondered: Mrs Loftheim has shown it all to me already. Surely there must be something else in Venice? But when he read on his father only wrote: *you won't have had an ice yet in Florian's?* He dropped the letter on the bed: there was nothing left except the conventional gestures, the 'love-froms' and the crosses which had been the nearest to a touch they had had during these years. Obediently he would repeat them back in his own letters, but he had forgotten what they meant: they were like hieroglyphs of an extinct tribe. The boy lay back and thought of Mr Hogan, and thinking of Mr Hogan he fell asleep.

The telephone woke him, and for a short time he couldn't think where he was: he thought it was somebody ringing the bell of his aunt's flat in Rome. It was quite dark in his room, and when he put out his fingers for the light he couldn't find it. Everything had moved around: even the window and the bed. Then he remembered that he was in Venice and this was – who?

He didn't recognise the voice, but more than a quarter of his life had passed since he last heard it. The voice said, 'Roger. Is that Roger?'

'Yes.'

'This is Daddy – your father.'

'Yes.'

'I've just got off the train. Are you awake, dear?'

'Yes.'

'Glad to see me?'

'Yes.'

'I shan't be very long now, but these gondolas charge too much. They want a thousand lira to the hotel. I'll catch the waterbus.'

'Yes.'

'We have to go all round the canal, so I'll be about half an hour. Starving?'

'No.'

'It'll be good to see you, old chap. I'll be off now.'

'Goodbye,' the child said politely and rang off. His watch said eight-fifteen, and curling his feet under him again he occupied his mind for a while with Mr Hogan. At eight-forty he heard the whistle of a waterbus and went to the window: the lamplit panes under their belt of black smoke went by: strangers stared out onto the canal and some looked up at the windows of the hotel where he stood – one of the strangers, he imagined, was his father. Fifty yards away at the San Marco jetty, the bus drew up, but by five to nine his father had not yet come. He had missed that bus, but there would be one (the air hostess had told him) every ten minutes, and for the next hour the boy stood there watching them go by – the same sounds and lights and faces and the same silence afterwards. Soon he began to cry with the sense of mystery rather than with the sense of fear or loneliness or bewilderment, but after a time he remembered that his nurse in the old days of a home had told him that a watched pot never boiled, so he lay down on his bed with his back to the window and the canal and counted the *vapori*, as they passed with his ears only, until, his face thrust down into the damp pillow, at last he fell asleep. While he slept, the lights in the hotel one by one went out in all the rooms, leaving only the gloomy light of passages, and presumably the last *vapore* went emptily by to its anchorage at two in the morning.

II

Major Court hung up the receiver with a dim feeling of disappointment. He had travelled from Trieste with mounting excitement. It was nearly three years since he had seen his son, and now that his wife had left him, the boy represented to him the whole of family life – that vaguely desired condition which he had never really enjoyed, that the War had broken for ever. (He never blamed his wife for what had happened: the War had broader shoulders on which to lay the blame for everything.) He hadn't been able to wait till he reached the hotel, but talking to his son on the telephone was like giving an unwanted present to somebody without the tact to pretend pleasure. He thought: 'Oh well, there are ten days' – ten days, he meant, in which to tie the two of them together, to re-establish a family. He was, he knew it himself, an incurable optimist.

The *vapore* lurched towards the pier, belching its smoke, unwashed and rusty. It was nearly low tide, and there was no grandeur in the green weedy foundations of the houses: they were for the connoisseurs of decay. This was something for which Major Court felt no appreciation. The peeling palaces, the rotted gondola posts, unused and wearing away between the level of the tides, the sense of a city sinking – he held these impressions obstinately at bay, standing in the bows in his too new civilian suit. Once he saw a rat scramble from the canal into a drain that the low tide had exposed, and he turned abruptly away and set up his position on the other side. Then he gazed out again seeing only what he was determined to see – a fine cast-iron lantern, a roof garden in the last sun, a beautiful Moorish façade. He stood there, looking one way, like an unbalanced expression of belief.

Perhaps he would have stayed there, staring out in safety at what he wanted to see all the way to San Marco, if he hadn't turned at the sound of an American voice referring to Lord Byron's Palazzo. He didn't think again about Lord Byron, because beyond the American he saw a back he felt certain he knew: hadn't he had the case of that particular narrow back and bent shoulders for quite a while in Trieste? He wondered what Peskovitch, if it really was Peskovitch, was doing in Venice. His men had seen to it that he was passed safely through to Rome, and there surely he should have stayed.

Major Court moved round until he could see the face... Yes – it was Peskovitch unquestionably. The momentary hesitation had been due, well, to the extraordinarily tired face, the look of surprise, and perhaps to the fact that for once he was without those steel-rimmed elderly spectacles. He had been in better condition after a prison camp and a journey without food for forty-eight hours across the mountains than he seemed to be in now. Major Court called across the deck to him, 'M. Peskovitch' (even in two days he had taken a fancy to the man) and saw Peskovitch's eyes blink short-sightedly back at him.

Major Court began to make his way beween the passengers. He said, 'How nice to see you again. You remember me – Court of the Venezia-Giulia police?' A voice said, 'There is some mistake. This is my great-uncle, Mario Varezi.'

For the first time Major Court noticed that Peskovitch – he could have sworn that it was Peskovitch – was accompanied. Two men were with him – the young man who spoke now and an elderly man with a weary grey moustache. They stood one on each side of – whoever it was – and Major Court was suddenly reminded of his first meeting with Peskovitch, who was brought into his office in Trieste between two policemen. 'He says his name is Peskovitch,' one of them had reported. Court asked with astonishment, 'Not *the* Peskovitch,' and heard the stranger reply in English, 'I suppose I was – last year.' 'He was reported dead.' 'I am the late Peskovitch,' the stranger had replied with humour and pride.

The other man said, 'It is not the first time this mistake has been made. M. Peskovitch seems to have a number of friends.'

'A great many,' Court said, watching the eyes of Varezi – if he was Varezi. The *vapore* swung in towards the Ca' d'Oro stop, and passengers pushed between them towards the side. Certainly in those tired dulled eyes there was nothing that could be taken for recognition. Again they were under way, lurching across to the next stop on the other side of the canal. Major Court said, 'I'm sorry. It is a startling likeness,' and moved away.

But he was worried: he tried to believe in Mario Varezi. He looked at his watch: half an hour had passed since he called his son, and he thought with unimaginative tenderness and anxiety: he'll be needing his dinner even if he isn't glad to see me. The Rialto bridge arched over them, and again there was a crush of passengers to the side. Only three more stops, he thought, and then family life began again: he would be a father and not an unwanted police officer working with strangers – and he started to plan the excursions they would do together, and presently, presently he would learn how to talk to a child. Three men moved together towards the gang plank.

Major Court told himself that this was none of his business: his business came to an end at the edge of the international zone. A man called Mario Varezi was no concern of his, and at the moment of the thought Varezi looked back, peered back short-sightedly, not with any trace of recognition or appeal, but with a puzzled air, as though Major Court did perhaps remind him of a face he had once seen a long time ago, in another life. Another life. This is the age of reincarnations. His elderly companion said something to Varezi, gently, leaning close to his ear, as though he did not want to draw the attention of the young man, who was pushing a way for them. Major Court quite suddenly decided that after all he was concerned. As the three men mounted the slope of the Rialto bridge and descended towards the fish market, Major Court followed fifty yards behind.

III

The shine of the jetty and the slap of the water marked the turning of the tide. In the clock tower by St Mark's the iron man beat out the hour of four, the east wind off the Adriatic carried the sound of his strokes down the first rank of the Grand Canal, just as it set the gondolas rocking on their rank outside the *Europa* Hotel. The noises entered the boy's dream and became the traffic of a railway station where he waited interminably for his father, while the trains went in and went out. A man in a Christmas mask took his hand and said, 'You're young Roger, aren't you? I'm going to give you a runaround.' 'Oh no, no,' he implored him. 'I must wait for my father,' but the man paid no attention, dragging him away from the platform towards a little dark doorway. 'You don't need to be scared of me,' he said, 'I've got a kid just like you. I'm Mr Hogan,' and the boy woke, sweating with his fear, and found that in the great glossy hotel room with the twin beds and the big mirrors there was only himself and all the shadows of the early hours.

Chapter two

Roger Court watched the police launch move in against the *Europa* jetty. The manager stood there ready to greet the police official who uncurled long weary legs from the cabin: a uniformed officer aided him ashore with a lift under the elbow. The manager put out a hand to take his briefcase but, with a sudden hop, skip and jump that reminded Roger Court of a grasshopper, the official was ashore. The boy went back into his room and sat on the unused bed and waited for the telephone to summon him. It was nearly midday: the police seemed as slow to arrive as a doctor when the layman considers a case serious.

The boy had finally woken at half-past seven and had lain in bed wondering what to do until eight. Then he had dressed and gone downstairs. At the reception desk he said, 'My father has not come.'

The clerk said, 'Oh, he'll be on the morning train, I expect.'

'No. He came last night. He telephoned to me from the station. I think he has been murdered.'

The clerk laughed. The boy said, 'Why didn't he come then?' and the clerk suddenly lost his laugh, leaving the smile baselessly in mid-air. 'Well,' he began, and then fled into the room behind to find the manager. The manager told him not to worry: they would see about everything: he was just to go on into the restaurant and have his breakfast. It was half-past eight. By nine o'clock the manager had decided unwillingly to telephone to the police.

But a man is not like a banknote. If a banknote is lost there is every reason to hurry on the search. If a man has been murdered he is safely out of circulation; sooner or later his body will turn up, in the canal or the lagoon; the earlier one begins to search, the earlier the undesirable publicity will start. And if – the more probable solution – he is alive, has only missed his train or spent his night in a brothel, the greater the delay, the more chance of keeping the whole affair from the newspapers for everybody's sake, even for the sake of the Press who never seem to realise that they are slowly strangling, with their stories of violence, this aged goose that for so many years had been laying its golden eggs.

The telephone rang and the boy lifted the receiver gingerly: he was not yet confident about which end was which, and he tried at first to speak through the earpiece. The manager said impatiently, 'Are you there, Mr Court?'

The boy got the receiver straight and said, 'But he hasn't turned up.'

'I mean you. Please come down to my office.'

The man in uniform opened the door for him. The long thin man drooped in an easy chair and the manager sat very upright at his desk. He said, 'The Commissioner wants to ask you a few questions.'

'Do you speak Italian?' The boy shook his head.

'I can translate for you,' the manager said.

'It is not necessary. I was a prisoner in England for four years.'

The boy said, 'Where's my father?'

The Commissioner said, 'Don't worry. Nobody can disappear in Venice – if he is in Venice.'

'But he is.'

'That has to be investigated.' He began to clean his nails with a toothpick. 'I have telephoned to Trieste. I have no evidence that he was ever on the train.'

'But I heard him, he spoke to me.'

'When did you last see him?'

'Three years ago.'

'How do you know it was he who spoke to you?'

'But it was. Of course it was. He said, "Is that you, Roger?" He asked if I'd had dinner. He said he would be with me in half an hour.'

'Did you recognise his voice?'

'His voice...' The boy began to cry: he had no idea what all this was about. Why should anyone pretend to be his father? That suggestion was more terrifying than his father's disappearance: it belonged to the world of Mr Hogan.

'It might have been anybody,' the Commissioner said. 'He may never have reached Venice.'

'But why? Why?'

The telephone rang. 'For you, Commissioner.'

The Commissioner said wearily, 'Yes. Yes. Oh, well... there might easily have been some mistake.' He rang off and asked the boy, 'Have you a photograph of your father?'

'No. But my aunt has.'

'Where is your aunt?'

'I don't know. She wrote her address down. She's gone to France on a holiday.' He began to feel in his pockets. Several scraps of paper came out – the newspaper photograph of an elephant, a recipe for making pistol caps at home, a code on which he had been working in private. He said dismally, 'I don't seem to have it.'

'She'll have to be told,' the manager said, 'if Major Court doesn't turn up today.'

'I suppose so,' the Commissioner said gloomily.

'She is in charge of the boy.'

'Is your mother dead?' the Commissioner asked.

'No.'

'Where is she?'

'I don't know.'

'You'd better turn out all your pockets.'

The collection on the desk grew: a lot of mottoes out of Perugina chocolates; a knife with a broken blade; the works of an old watch; a Boy Scouts Diary for 1939.

'Did you write it in there?' the Commissioner asked.

'No. It's on a bit of paper.'

But the bit of paper was nowhere. The last pocket produced only a wisp of tissue paper wrapped round a grey pebble the size of a pea.

'What's that?' the Commissioner asked with interest, as though he would like to change the whole course of the investigation to a more appealing subject.

'Something for making gunpowder.'

'What's it called?'

'Nobody knows. I call it ingredient X2.'

The manager impatiently interrupted them. 'But there must be some way of getting in touch with your aunt.'

'I don't know.'

'Didn't she tell you where she was going?'

'Something beginning with Sainte…'

'Well, run along now,' the Commissioner told him with a slight sigh, as though really they two could have got along better by themselves without the other policeman and the manager, certainly without the case that lay so heavily on all their hands. He began to help the boy shovel the objects back into his pockets. When he reached the diary he paused. 'This seems a little out of date.'

'The tables aren't.'

'You mean weights and measures?'

'International Morse,' the boy said.

'Yes, of course. That's useful. I wish I had learnt it myself.'

'You don't know Morse?'

'No.'

The boy said reluctantly, 'I might be able to lend it to you for a few days.'

'I will borrow it when I have time.'

Standing in the doorway, the boy appealed to all of them. 'But my father?...'

The Commissioner said, 'Oh, he will turn up. You may be sure. If not today, tomorrow. You will hear from him. There is nothing to worry about. Nothing.' He held out a hundred lira note. 'Buy yourself some sweets.'

'I have enough, thank you.' The boy shut the door behind him. He was an adept at detecting false comfort.

The light from the water danced in the mirrors, and the pale furniture of the lounges glowed like honey in the sun. He walked through room after empty room, his rubber soles squeaking on the parquet, and for the first time he missed the loud friendly voices of the Americans who had such a capacity for just filling space. Now space stretched all round him with nothing to fill it but himself, and the loneliness and the fears loped on his track, like unknown beasts who were waiting till nightfall to approach. It would not be long before a whole day had passed since his father had said down the telephone, 'Half an hour.' That was a fact not even a policeman could avoid:

71

there was no safe or happy explanation that he could find. A waiter in a white coat went by him from the bar carrying drinks towards the manager's office.

The boy came out on the jetty. The police launch had gone off on some other errand. He heard voices and recognised them, and realised that he was close to the window of the manager's office; they spoke in Italian and he could only understand a few words here and there. Once he heard 'no evidence' and once 'we shall try the hospitals'. He could hear the sound of glasses laid down on the desk and the sound made him feel as though he and his father were completely forgotten.

II

Although it was the hottest hour of the afternoon, a candle burning in a bottle gave the only light inside the little cavernous wine shop. The boy peered in and moved off down the street. He had crossed the Rialto bridge for no reason that he knew and, making his way past the stalls into the Ruga Vecchia San Giovanni, had stared up one of the dark narrow side streets where the sun never came. The houses on either side leaned for support on the arches above his head. He walked as though in sleep, with no rational aim: two fingers of his left hand were crossed for luck, and every thirteen paces he changed step and at every seventh doorway he paused and looked within. He used every charm he knew and invented others: by this means he had a faint hope that he might see his father.

He tried to remember what his father looked like. His aunt's photograph had been taken more than twenty years ago, when his father was a very young man, and it bore no resemblance to the middle-aged stranger who had bid goodbye to him two and a half years ago. He had been five and a few months then – a child, and he was a little embarrassed to think of the way his father would have remembered him – sitting in that green toy motor car on the gravel path of the Laurels. His father had shaken hands with him and said, 'So long, old chap, so long,' and suddenly bending down and blowing the smell of beer and cigarette smoke into his face before kissing him roughly and quickly and shamefacedly on the forehead. Then his father had moved off down the path to the gate, limping a little from his bad left leg: he had sounded his horn, and his father had turned and waved, and he had released his brake and got his feet ready on the pedals with the intention of a quick rush towards his father – one of his record-breaking Brooklands[2] rushes just to show his father the daring of which he was capable, but he had become aware of his mother watching from a window, and he took his feet from the pedals and ran indoors. So now he could remember nothing but a limp and a clean-shaven face.

Through every seventh doorway he peered for a clean-shaven man with a limp: he listened for any English words: his ears read into the creak of timber or the cry of a child a call for help. When he reached the Rio delle Beccarie, he peered into the water expecting to see a clean-shaven face washing by with the old tins and the garbage. He felt no grief at the idea of his father's death, but he was aware of his own loneliness and fear in this city of strangers, and he was sorry for his father because he was in the same case. It seemed to him that this was a situation that his mother should have shared, and he blamed her for not being there.

One, two, three, four, five, six, seven – a courtyard of tall, dirty tenements and the washing hanging right across from every floor like flags that have been left out too long after a triumphal parade. Two men were talking in the yard – an elderly man with a drooping moustache shook his head and said in Italian, 'sick, very sick,' and the other commiserated with him – on the illness of his wife? His son? His friend? 'It is fortunate you are a doctor,' the boy could understand that much. The doctor saw him watching and came towards him with an air of gentle kindliness. He was very thin, so thin that his trousers hung in ungainly folds around his legs and his wrists were as slight as a woman's. Once Mr Hogan had prepared a bath of lime for Major Ronnie Dunne; 'In a few hours,' he had said, 'you will be a skeleton.' It was as if the bath in the doctor's case had been interrupted.

He took in the boy's foreign clothes and asked him if he were lost, and suddenly – at the sound of the word 'lost' – the boy realised that in fact he had no idea of how to regain the Rialto bridge. The word haunted him, the gentle sympathetic face in this word of Mr Hogan's moved him, so that the tears became heavy behind the eyes. He nodded his head.

'You are American?'

'English,' he said.

'Where do you want to go?'

'To the Rialto.'

'But where are you staying?'

The boy became suddenly secret and said, 'I can get the waterbus there.'

'Where is your mother?' and for no particular reason at all – except perhaps that he was tired of answering that particular question with the confession that he did not know – he said, 'At the hotel.'

'Which hotel?'

He lied again with the first name that came into his head. 'The *Grand*.'

The doctor put out his hand and said, 'I will show you the way,' and he felt the doctor's fingers placed like a bundle of pencils in his palm. They walked in silence, and the boy no longer counted or changed his step: he was aware of the depressing truth that adults carried round with them – there was no such thing as magic. The doctor said suddenly, 'Do you like ice cream?'

'Yes.'

'There is a café near here: a clean café – one has to be careful in this place because of the water.' The boy swam a little in his wake like a dinghy: he had no longer any will of his own. The last hope of finding his father himself had vanished with the magic: loneliness lay like ballast in his stomach. 'You must tell your mother to be careful – not to drink water out of taps.' He sat the boy down at a table and called 'Luigi. A chocolate ice.' He explained to the boy, 'Chocolate is more healthy. Vanilla is all right, but it is not so nourishing as food, and the fruit ices are all chemical.'

The boy pursued his own train of thought: he recognised kindliness sitting there on a little iron chair with an empty plate watching him eat. 'You could manage another?'

He drew a deep breath and said, 'I told you a lie.'

'A lie.'

'I am not staying at the *Grand* Hotel. I am staying at the *Europa*.'

'You are a strange boy,' the doctor said. Though he had led him by the hand to this place, he talked to him like a grown man. He said, 'I have never been married and I have no children. You see, my health was not good enough. One must not pass on one's sickness. Why did you lie?'

'You asked too many questions.'

'Yes, yes. I see. That is what it is to be a doctor. One gets used to asking, "Is the pain here or there?" I live with sickness and we ask the sick questions.'

'Do you work in a hospital?'

'You see – you ask questions too. No, I have private patients. I worked in a hospital once when I was a young man. That was a long time ago.'

The boy scraped round and round his glass. He said, 'Do your patients die?'

'Sometimes.'

'Have you any dying now?'

'I don't know. I have two bad cases of typhoid – the water again. Perhaps they will recover. Perhaps not. Please have another ice.'

The boy said, 'I told two lies. My mother isn't here.'

'Ah. It's your father who is looking after you?'

'My aunt sent me here to meet him.'

'You have no mother?'

'She has gone away.'

The doctor said quickly, 'And you love your father? There you see how it is – asking questions again. Always asking questions.'

Sucking his spoon, the boy looked up at him, a careful scrutiny. 'I don't mind,' he said. He took another suck and another look. 'I don't know where he is.'

'You have lost each other,' the doctor said. 'Venice is difficult for strangers. You should go back to your hotel. He will be anxious. You will find him there.' It was like a promise.

'Yes,' the boy said and rose.

III

But the promise was not fulfilled. His father had not come. The clerk at the desk said, 'We have had to move your room. We will give you a big room again when your father comes.' He showed the boy into the lift and, as they rose, he tried to encourage him. 'The police are trying to trace your aunt. They have telegraphed to the *Sûreté* in Paris.' But surely it was his father they should be trying to trace.

His new room was very small, with heavy old-fashioned furniture. Workmen swung on a platform outside his window preparing the façade of the hotel for the season. He was out of sight of the canal, and there were no passing *vapori* now to remind him that his father was not on board. For a while he stood and watched the workmen – there was nothing else to do, except to look again at the paper he had already read more than once. When he searched for it in the attaché case which somebody had packed for him, he found that he hadn't even that to fall back upon – the paper was missing. He amused himself for a while opening the cupboard doors and testing the walls for secret hiding places where somebody might at some time have left a message or even a piece of stolen jewellery, but he was unsuccessful. A bell by the bed was marked with some pictures of the people who would come at a call: a man dragging a trunk, a maid with a broom, a waiter with a tray, and his hand hovered for a moment over the three buttons. Then he went into the bathroom, filled the bath and tried to construct, with the help of a loose piece of wood from the cupboard, a waterfall down which a man might shoot in a barrel or a tooth glass. It was very unconvincing and, when the floor was uncomfortably awash, he stopped. He hadn't really wanted to play that game. It was as if all the time he was keeping something at bay.

Back in the bedroom it occurred to him that he might organise a race between the maid, the porter and the waiter. He counted his money and, finding that he had exactly five hundred lira, he betted himself five to one that the waiter would win. He put his stake – a hundred-lira note – under the ashtray and with scrupulous justice used the palm of his hand to press all three buttons simultaneously.

He was out of luck – the maid and the porter arrived simultaneously. He could tell from their attitude that they would not appreciate his motive, so he told them that he had rung by mistake. The porter left at once with an air of not liking children: the maid lingered sympathetically until a thin trickle of water emerged from under the bathroom door. He had forgotten to turn off the tap. Luckily she could speak no English, but the clatter she made in mopping up the water expressed her feelings, and he felt it wisest not to ask her (as he had intended) to find his magazine and some notepaper. He would have been at a complete loss if he had not found at the back of a drawer, so cunningly concealed in the bureau that one might almost have classed it as a secret one, a small stub of white chalk. With this he was able to construct on the floor the materials for a game of cricket. A large circle enclosed a lot of numbers and penalties. He only had to choose two teams and then, by throwing the chalk into the circle, find the score. He captained one team, putting himself in to bat third man and thus providing backbone to his side – very luckily, as a boy called Droopy was LBW[3] first ball. His team made 110.

When it came to choosing the second team, he put his head against the side of the bed and began to cry: loneliness and fear had returned in his attempt to write down his father's name as captain. Some day the police would trace his aunt and she would arrive and fetch him – a woman's world would enclose him again. He knew for the first time that he had wanted to see his father. He didn't hear the two knocks on the door, and he only became aware that he was not alone by seeing two feet standing on the cricket scores. 'Allo,' a voice said. The boy raised his head and saw the waiter as though he was coming down a long road towards him through a blur of rain: an ugly, cheerful, savage face with a big crooked nose and the appearance of a sailor rather than a servant.

'Allo,' he said again. 'You're the kiddo' (he used some extraordinary words). The boy said nothing, letting the tears run – there was no point now in trying to hide them.

'Well, say something,' the waiter said in a tone that could easily have been mistaken for fury. 'You rang, didn't you? I came hoity presto. What do you want, eh?'

It was as though in his misery he had slipped back two years. He whimpered at the waiter, 'My father.'

'And can I find him for you?' the waiter demanded. 'You have to leave that to the police. No? What?'

'They'll never find him,' the boy said.

The waiter squatted down on his haunches beside the boy, and raising the bedcover peeped under the bed. 'Are we alone?'

'I think so.'

'Have you searched the cupboard?'

'Yes,' the boy said and suddenly grinned.

'Fine, fine,' the waiter said, 'leave everything to me. What is that game you are playing?'

'Cricket.'

'But where is the bat and the ball and the stakes?'

'Stumps.'

'Stumps, then.'

The boy began to explain and the waiter threw the chalk. It landed on a six and he clapped his hands with pleasure. 'I was the best batter in the camp.'

'Were you a prisoner?'

'Yes.'

'So was the Commissioner of Police.'

'Ah, but not like me. I fought to the last round. I killed dozens. Even the enemy cheered me when I was carried in full of bullets.'

'Have you got a lot of scars?'

'No. Now the surgeons are very clever. They sew you up without any scars.' He threw the chalk again, and it landed on the letter C. 'What does that mean?'

'Caught.' The waiter threw the chalk impatiently away. 'This is not real cricket. In real cricket I was never catched. I would smote the ball over the border.'

'Boundary.' The boy had forgotten to cry. He was no longer alone. He felt an enormous sense of trust – here was someone who would give him a straight answer. 'Will the police find my father?'

The waiter said, 'They will be ringing for me. I have been up and down to this floor all day. I call it the thirsty floor.' His eyes seemed to beseech the boy not to repeat his question. He said, 'I must be going,' and at the same time he sat down on the edge of the bed and touched the boy's hair. 'What's your name?'

'Roger.'

'Mine is Roberto Salvini.'

'Will they find my father?'

The waiter said, 'There is always hope.' It was the most hopeless thing he could say. He went on, 'You have got to know these things, and there is no one here who will tell you. A man – a foreigner – disappeared from Rome nearly a week ago. He was recognised on the Venezia train, but the police here have not found him yet. It did not matter so much – he was a refugee from Yugoslavia. Now your father has disappeared. It looks bad. They wish it not happened at all. They would like to prove that it not happened here.'

'I don't understand.'

'They say he must have disappeared from the train. I listen to them, you know, when I carry in the drinks.'

'But he spoke to me.'

'They say *somebody* spoke to you.'

He rose from the bed and said, 'They will be ringing and ringing. Listen. We will meet at six. I have the evening off. We will have a drink together. Things are not so bad if you have a friend.'

'Please,' the boy said, 'will you find my father, Roberto?'

The waiter pulled the lobe of the boy's ear – once, twice, three times. 'Why not?' he said. 'Why not? A little thing like that.'

Chapter three

Roberto ordered himself another vermouth, and a second ice cream for the boy. He said, 'It would be more easy if you had a photograph.' The evening crowd filled the narrow street off the piazza, and the boy stared through the windows of the café at the swim of faces that moved as slowly as fish in a tank; sometimes they hung suspended for a while outside, staring back.

'We have to make sure, you see, that he did arrive.'

'I know that. He spoke to me. I told you so.'

'But, kiddo, you see, we must make the police admit it is true. Then they will have to search properly. Now they say it was not him who spoke.'

'Can't you find him without them?'

'Well, maybe, yes. Roberto can do the hell of a lot of things. One day I tell you some of them, but today, kiddo, I would rather the police helped. Now you just describe your father to me. Make believe he is sitting here just beside you. Would he have a moustache?'

'I don't know.'

'Is he tall?'

'Yes. No.'

'But kiddo, he can't be both.'

The child's eyes filled with tears as though a mere hint of impatience was a threat of dissension. 'He's taller than you.'

'Now we're getting somewhere. He must be a fine big man if he's bigger than Roberto.'

The child said with nodding solemnity, 'There he is.'

Roberto swung quickly round. 'Where?'

The child said, 'He went by the window.'

'You're joking,' but the child's face answered for him that he hardly knew the word. 'Quick,' Roberto said, 'we must to catch him.' He called out something to the waiter in Italian and dragged the boy through the door. 'Which way?'

'Right,' but when Roberto began to pull him that way the child hung back.

'No, the other.'

'One day somebody's got to teach you a lot, kiddo,' Roberto said. They pushed their way together through the evening crowd. Outside each café they paused and peered within. 'You were not just imagining things, were you?' Roberto asked.

'I saw him,' the boy said with confidence.

'How did you know him? Did you see his face plain?'

'I didn't see his face. There,' the child said, 'there, there he goes,' but in spite of his words he had to be dragged by Roberto in the wake of the limping man, as though already he realised that all men who limped were not his father; he had not really needed the explosion of excited Italian when Roberto seized the man by the shoulder to learn that.

'Now what made you say that to me?' Roberto complained, watching the indignant municipal councillor limp away.

'It was the way he walked.'

Roberto raised his hands indignantly. 'Of all the stupid things I have done, to pick a kiddo like you,' but suddenly, seizing the boy in a friendly painful way by the ear, he said, 'You mean your father – he had a limp like that?'

'Yes.'

'And why do you keep so many secrets from your friend Roberto? Maybe your father he has a long white beard and no teeth: maybe he is a very fat man: maybe he has a stammer. Maybe he is a giant or a dwarf, like Luza.'

The boy shook his head.

'Well,' Roberto said, 'that is fine to get along with. We know something now – we can look for a man. He has a limp. Now, does he limp this way or that way?' and Roberto, finding a few feet of freedom in the crowded street, imitated a limp first with the right, then with the left foot.

'That way – I think,' the boy said, trying to make out the way his father walked out of his life down the gravel path.

'Was he wounded in the War?'

'I don't know.'

'You not know where your mother is, you not know what your father looks like – you lead a strange life, kiddo,' but he could never have convinced the boy of that: there is no strangeness where there is no companion. This was his only life, and he led it the only way he could. He said, 'Have *you* got a father?'

'Oh, a mighty fine one. When he was young he could knock down a bullock – so.'

'And a mother?'

'*Bellissima*. She had ten children before she was lucky and had me.'

They had reached the café, and sitting at the table they had left was the smallest man the child had ever seen – he was an inch shorter than himself and he had little beady belligerent eyes. He was drinking a glass of wine, but he gave an impression of holding it in his palm so only the better to fling it in an enemy's face. The grudge he had against the world was as old as his birth. He said to Roberto in Italian, 'You are late. I have many appointments.' He wore a peaked cap like a soldier, and he glared at the child as though he would gladly have put him to the sword: it was as if he had measured his height and took the extra inch for an insult.

'This is the kiddo.' The two men talked for a long while in Italian and the boy picked up only a word here and there – especially the word 'police' repeated often with venom. Presently Roberto said to the boy, 'This is Giorgio Luza. He take the tickets for the waterbus. I have asked him whether he remembers a lame man buying a ticket after the train came in from Trieste.'

'Does he remember?'

'He says he is too busy to remember things like that.'

'It isn't any use then?'

'Ah, but you see, he has a great hatred for the Commissioner. That is why I asked him to come. He is prepared to tell the Commissioner that he saw your father. The Commissioner will not be pleased. He will have to do things now. He will have to search the city. There will be a lot of publicity and if he does not find your father it will be very bad for him.'

It was too complicated for the child. He only said: 'I wish he had really seen my father.'

They walked back in silence towards the hotel. It was dark, and the pigeons had left the square: it was long past bedtime. The little venomous dwarf moved in the boy's imagination – in the stories he had read, the hero never had such allies. Why couldn't it have been the Commissioner who helped him – that tall, lazy man who had spoken to him quite so kindly? Under the little humped bridge which they had to cross a gondolier slid rapidly by, his long boat gleaming into the lamplight and out again like a water serpent. Roberto said, 'One moment, kiddo.'

He led the boy into the shadowiness of a great empty church. Two old women prayed by a side altar and one ragged figure stood in front of the crucifix on the high altar, giving the bowed figure a long straight stare back like an equal. Roberto said softly, 'One has only a small small belief, but it does no harm to try everything.' He crossed the church and stood before the statue of St Anthony, the meaningless figure with the child in his arms, the utility saint so useful for lost keys and lost sweethearts. 'Go on,' Roberto said, 'pray to him. Ask him to find your father.'

'I'm not a Roman Catholic,' the boy said. He was scared of the shadows, the suggestion of magic, the obscure doings of the old women with candles.

'That is not important,' Roberto said with a kind of contempt. 'He finds things for everybody, even Germans. Go on. Tell him you will make an offering.' The boy had no idea what an offering was, and he knew he was not good at making things, but he had to obey, if Roberto considered that it might work. He whispered, 'Please St Anthony, find my father and I will make an offering.' When he turned, Roberto for a moment was not in his sight, and the fear of desertion came over him again, and he put his fingers to his mouth in a gesture he hadn't used for four years.

Then he saw Roberto turning away from a statue of God's Mother. Roberto held his hand as they left the church. The boy asked him, 'Did you pray too?'

Roberto said, 'One never knows,' in a tone of sombre hope.

'Did you pray that we'd find my father?'

Roberto looked down at the boy and pressed his hand more tightly. Children belonged to the world; they could not be hidden from it. He said, 'I prayed that we might find him alive, kiddo.'

Part Two

Chapter one

'One must take things as they are, Major Court,' the doctor said, moving his thin arm with the rolled-up sleeve as though he would indicate how things were: the damp and airless room, the kitchen chairs, the occasional table with the remains of marquetry that had known better days. The basin of water, the towel, the syringe, the torn mattresses – you could hardly distinguish the human form on one of them from the grey army blankets. Major Court stood at the locked window and watched far below a gondola pass by, laden with ash cans. It was early morning and the hour for sewage. The empty tins bobbed in the dark water like fishes. It was preferable to the sight of the small crowded room and the two men dozing against the wall with their guns in their laps.

'I don't believe in the inevitable,' Major Court said. It occurred to him that it was a strange hour and place for philosophical argument, for the kind of opening gambit that he might have played as a young don in the senior common room after a good dinner in the days before the second War. One of the two men coughed without waking: he had done it all through the night.

'Like Pascal,' the doctor said, 'I put my trust in the greatest probability.'

'Will he die?' Major Court asked, nodding at the grey blanket.

'Almost certainly.' Major Court tried to detect the breathing under the blankets, but there seemed no more life there than a rag doll has.

'Oh, not of this,' the doctor said, making a little movement of his hand as though it still held a syringe, 'or here, but there, you know, over there.'

Major Court stared down into the canal. There was nothing to see outside that he hadn't made a note of long ago – how long ago? For some reason of their own they had taken away his watch, and it was difficult to keep count of time. He supposed they were calculating on that: to be without the measurement of time was an effective minor torture: it made the days interminable. 'You may be miscalculating the probabilities,' he said.

'Of course. Like Pascal. But the stake on one side is so much greater. One can count on the mercy of – the other side.'

'I doubt it now. We've learnt a good deal and we've picked up a lot of – bad manners. Remember Nuremberg.'

'Oh well...' The doctor sighed. Certainly, Major Court thought, his choice of probability had not made him happy – it hadn't even made him prosperous or fat. 'Would you mind rolling up your sleeve, Major Court?'

'You agreed there was no harm in waiting till morning.'

'It's half-past five.'

'I wouldn't have known. I haven't got a watch.'

'We'll wait another half hour if you like. I know you have an idea that the police will find you – oh, they'll probably begin searching in a day or two, but we'll have moved by then.'

'You think it will work on me as effectively...'

'A rather larger dose perhaps.'

'He was a good man,' Major Court said, looking at the bed. 'Won't you feel rather bad when he's disposed of?'

'Of course, but I shall persuade myself that if it hadn't been me who helped them, it would have been another. For your people have not left us a livelihood. There are always unemployed – technicians – like myself to be used.'

'Your belief in the inevitable again. History's against you. Even recent history.'

'The inevitable is sometimes postponed. It was postponed in 1815, 1918 and 1945. The process goes on. Do you know Venice, Major Court?

'Not well.'

'Look out of the window. You see how high the water rises on the steps. Venice is sinking an inch into the lagoon every hundred years. Already once a year at the highest tide you can take a gondola into the square of St Mark's. In six hundred years the water will be all over the floor of the cathedral. It will be abandoned. Presently we shall float over it in our boats and see the dome like a great barnacle below the keel.' It was the doctor's favourite theme. He never tired of that particular simile – it sounded to him like literature. The thin fingers made gestures of seaweed indicating the end of everything lovely. Major Court remembered the rat he had seen climb out of the canal and disappear into a drain. The smell of decay blew up from the canal. 'That is what I mean by the inevitable,' the doctor said.

'One can never tell,' Major Court replied. 'Some engineer might invent something...' It sounded a weak argument even to his own ears.

'And just so,' the doctor concluded. 'Your world. My world is sinking.'

'One can only do what one can.'

'I respect you, Major Court. I wish you had never seen us with Peskovitch on the waterbus. Or if only you had not followed. Now I can do nothing but obey orders. I am trying to persuade them to leave you here when they take him away. You can't cause any trouble after this.' He began to wash his syringe in the basin.

'I am not quite convinced that I ought not to make a fight.'

'What's the good? We should have to shoot.'

'The shot might be heard.' The doctor didn't even bother to answer him: they had been over that point so many times. It was really a kind of mercy they were showing him. If the authorities on the other side wanted him shipped across for interrogation (for some reason they seemed convinced that, just because he knew Peskovitch, he belonged to some branch of intelligence), he could be moved the more easily and comfortably. If he had to be eliminated, he would never know the moment of death – and, of course, there was always hope. It was only those who believed in the inevitable who were not handcuffed sooner by that theological virtue.

'How quickly does it work?' Major Court asked.

'A matter of seconds. At first you will just sleep…'

'Does the brain ever recover?' It was strange standing there doing nothing, watching the drug prepared that would turn him presumably into such an automaton as Peskovitch had become, so that he had not even recognised his name when he had addressed him, standing between two strangers on the waterbus.

'Of course, of course,' the doctor said reassuringly, as though he were talking to a patient. A terrible languor fell over Major Court's spirits. He said, 'In a way I shall be glad to sleep. He isn't the worst worry. There's my boy…'

'No harm can come to him.'

'I know that. But I don't like the idea of his loneliness… I suppose he's back with his aunt by now. I would have liked seeing him again.'

'You mustn't despair, Major Court.'

The doctor was washing his hands now. Usually, before an operation, one had the comforting sense of benevolence: one submitted to the anaesthetist with confidence that all was for the best, even though the worst might happen. In this dirty room, four floors up over the dingy branch canal, where the dozing man coughed and coughed over his old army revolver, there was no confidence in anything at all.

'Do you mind pulling up your sleeve, Major Court?' As the doctor advanced with his syringe Major Court thought, 'Is this really the inevitable, is this the shabby future for us all?'

Chapter two

The boy didn't know why he was there, for nobody seemed to require him. He had been fetched by the consulate motor boat and now sat in the Commissioner's office listening to the veiled insolences that went back and forth between the grown-up men.

The British Consul – a short man with a breezy commercial manner and astute brown eyes – said, 'Of course, Commissioner, I realise you know your business best, but a British subject has been missing for three days now... I don't want a Peskovitch case involving one of us, though what possible motive...'

'You know as well as I do, Mr Harrington, that one must begin a case at the beginning. I had no evidence that Major Court was even in Venice...'

'He had promised to meet his son that night and he telephoned from the station.'

'Somebody telephoned. I have been trying to trace the Major's movements from the Trieste end. I have had very little cooperation. Naturally, at the same time, I have been trying to pick up traces of him in the city. We have our sources.'

'Again I realise you have greater experience than I have in these matters, Commissioner, but I should have thought a house-to-house search, at least in the more dubious areas, the docks, behind the fish market.'

'It's not a thing one undertakes lightly. Until we had this evidence of the limping man, I wasn't prepared...'

'But I take it now you are going ahead with your habitual energy?'

'We are starting behind the docks and sealing off the canals round every block. We shall need the child with us – that's why I asked you to bring him. There's nobody else who can identify Major Court. Tomorrow we shall take another area.'

The Consul lowered his voice, and the boy, knowing that secrets were being spoken, leant back in his corner, with his eyes shut, intently listening. 'Careful nothing unpleasant,' were the words he caught.

'I have children of my own, Mr Harrington.'

'Yes,' the Consul said. He turned dubiously to the boy and said, 'Roger.' The boy opened his eyes. 'The police want you to help them. You won't be afraid to go with them in one of their boats, will you?'

'No.'

'They are very fine boats – speedboats. Latest type. You will be interested in the engines.'

'Yes.'

'When you come back, I want you to come and stay with us at the consulate. I have a boy not much older than you. You'll get on well together,' he added dubiously. 'It will be better than the hotel until we can find your aunt.'

The boy began to cry silently in his corner, the tears swelling like blisters in the corner of his eyes and bursting between the lids.

'I expect you are lonely at the hotel,' the Consul said. The boy shook his head.

'You aren't scared of us, are you?' the Consul asked with timidity. He wished this hadn't happened in front of the Commissioner, who watched the scene like an outsider who could have done better. The boy said obscurely through his tears, 'But Roberto...'

'What's that?'

But what was the good, the child thought, of using that name here. None of them knew Roberto. Nobody knew that only Roberto had the wit and courage to find his father. Nobody in this room of strangers knew that loneliness only now beginning.

Chapter three

The first day the police searched the area of the docks without result. At ten-thirty in the morning of the second day they closed the Rialto bridge, unwillingly: that was something you couldn't keep out of the papers. A routine search in dockland was of little interest, but there are no editors in the world who couldn't find room for a paragraph that contained the name Rialto. A whole quarter behind the Rialto was sealed off: on two sides the Grand Canal, and on the other two those narrow waterways, the Rio delle Beccarie and the Rio dei Meloni. In that dark sunless network of streets, the people seethed like disturbed flies round a pile of ordure. Shoppers who had come from outside to the fish market found themselves forbidden to recross the bridges, and men of dubious profession who were always uncertain of police motives retired discreetly into their kitchens and became helpful to their wives. The *vapori* did not call that morning at the Rialto pier, and the police patrols pressed steadily inwards between the canals, checking papers.

The boy sat in the police launch by the Rialto pier. The men who yesterday were amused and interested by his presence were today rather bored and irritated. They had worked off all their vicarious paternal feelings, and now were aware only of the impediment he represented. They could not tell how much Italian he understood, and they were prevented from joking freely. A tired constraint hung over the launch, and its shadow crept over the boy. He fidgeted, unable to sit still. That awful sense of loving nobody – the dark night of maturity – touched him prematurely. Did it matter, he wondered, whether they found his father? Who was his father, a man with a limp?

A policeman signalled from the bridge and one of the men said sharply to the boy, 'They want you over there.'

'What for?'

'Perhaps they've found your father.'

He half-recognised the streets they led him down – he thought perhaps that on that first day of fear and action he had been there before. That was when he still felt love. Now he shuffled in the policeman's wake, a small and loveless figure who was tired and wanted to go home and forget the whole thing.

In the gateway of a tenement block a police officer waited. 'Come along,' he said. 'I want you with me.' He explained. 'Upstairs there are two sick men who arrived the night your father disappeared. I want you to have a look at them.'

A group of them moved up the stairs together: a long steep climb. On the second floor a man opened a door, saw them and closed it hurriedly: they paid him no attention, moving up. 'Stay here,' the officer told the boy, just before they topped the last landing, and, when he did not immediately obey, the officer stamped his foot and said furiously, 'I said stay.' The boy stopped.

He heard the officer knock at the door, but he couldn't see him because of the top step. The officer had to knock twice. Then he heard the door open and a muddle of Italian voices, the shuffle of feet and silence. He sat down on the stairs and put his head in his hands, and felt tired and very old. He thought, to encourage himself, 'There's Roberto. Later I will see Roberto,' but on this grey damp Venetian morning he felt no love even for Roberto. He was empty. A voice called to him, 'Come.'

He came through the door. He saw that the officer's holster was undone, but the gun had not been drawn. The doctor stared at him with astonishment. 'Why, little one…'

'Do you know each other?' the officer asked the boy. All the men seemed perturbed by the unexpected. The boy nodded.

'Where did you meet?'

'He gave me an ice cream.'

'What were you doing?'

'He had lost his way,' the doctor explained, 'and was frightened.'

'I was looking for my father,' the boy said.

'Why him?' the officer asked.

'I was just looking.'

'Look again then,' the officer said. He was suspicious now that there was something he did not understand. He went across to the mattresses. 'Look at these men. Is one of them your father?' The doctor moved his hand nervously. He was leaning against the table, and now he put his hand on the book he had been reading, Spengler's *Decline of the West*,[4] as though to draw from the very feel of the book confidence in the inevitable.

The boy looked down at a man under a blanket: the thin elderly features of a stranger. He said, 'That's not my father.'

'And this one?' the officer asked.

'They are very sick,' the doctor said. 'I would pray you not to disturb them.'

'Is this your father?' the officer asked.

The boy looked down at a second stranger: a man with a coarse three days' growth of beard dressed in an old striped shirt open at the neck. This was like yesterday – they showed him all the wrong people. 'No,' he said. The doctor looked at the floor which shifted, and then moved firmly back into place.

But with something the officer was not satisfied – perhaps it was only a quality in the doctor's silence: perhaps he had protested too much, or not enough. The officer laid his hand on the shirt and tried to shake the stranger awake.

The doctor said, 'You have no right... You have seen their papers. You hear what the boy says.' The officer shook the man again and the eyes opened.

'Look again,' the officer commanded, and the boy looked with revulsion at the unwashed face and the three days' dirt. The stranger's eyes were trying to focus on him like a drunkard's.

'Of course he's not my father,' the boy said, and the stranger's hand moved at the sound of the English words.

'Please,' the doctor implored, but the officer paid him no attention, turning with vexation sharply to the door.

The doctor watched the man's eyes trying to focus. The lips were moving and as the door closed the doctor thought he could make out the first syllable of a boy's name before the hand fell hopelessly back and the lids shut again on whatever vague vision the brain had registered of his small son moving away.

II

The waiter said uneasily, 'But kiddo, you shouldn't have come.' The boy sat very upright in a recess of the great smart lounge, and Roberto stood over him, tray in hand.

'I wanted to see you,' the boy said sullenly.

'But how did you manage it?'

'They gave me money for sweets,' he said. 'I got on the *vapore*.'

'You are better off at the consulate.'

'No.'

'They are kind to you, aren't they?'

'Yes. I hate Morgan.'

'Who's Morgan?'

'The boy there. He thinks he can order me around. He's jealous because I went out on the police boat. He says I'm soft.' This was the longest statement the boy had made since he came to Venice: it was as if something inside him were breaking up with pain and letting the words out. '*Cameriere, cameriere,*' somebody called, and Roberto went off with the tray. The boy watched patiently the door through which he had disappeared. He didn't move an inch, not even his eyes, till Roberto came back.

Roberto put a glass of orange juice before the boy and stared. 'You mustn't mind him, kiddo.'

'Roberto,' the boy said, 'can't we find my father without all of them?'

'They are trying to help,' Roberto said.

'They are so stupid – the people they showed me. None of them was like my father. And tomorrow it will happen all over again.'

'There is sense in it, kiddo. You can't hide a man in Venice. If he has been kidnapped, they will find him.'

The wail of a siren rose over the canals and bridges and descended behind the domes. 'Come quickly,' Roberto said, 'and you will see a sight, kiddo.' He pulled him out onto the jetty, and with a roar and an insolent rush they came, a troop of six scarlet speedboats, setting the gondolas flapping on their moorings, rocking the jetty with the wave of their passing, a gleam of nozzles and helmets. Boatmen rowed wildly to clear a path, and a man in the first speedboat waved his hand and called something out to the boy, but it was lost in the roar and the wash of their passage.

'Fire practice,' Roberto said.

The boy's lips were wet with longing. He said, 'Morgan says they are the best boats on the canal – better than the police boats.'

'Yes.'

'Morgan went on a practice once. His father fixed it.'

'When we've found your father,' Roberto said, 'he will fix anything for you.'

'I want to stay here, Roberto.'

'But you can't, kiddo. It's past your dinner time. They will be anxious. If they find you here talking to me… Oh, mercy sakes,' Roberto said, 'what an imbroglio.'

'I want to be here.'

'The Consul is a good man.'

'I ought to be here. My father might telephone to me here.'

'He will know where to find you. They will tell him.'

'Has the Consul got a telephone?'

'Of course he has.'

'But, Roberto, if they don't find him we must do it.'

'Listen, kiddo. I'm going to ask the manager for permission to take you home.'

'It isn't home.'

'Be good, kiddo, and we will stop off on the way and meet a friend of mine. Roberto has not been idle. Roberto has found out a few things.'

'Not that little man?'

'No. Somebody else.'

'He scares me. He's wicked.'

'We will not have to see him again. He has done what we wanted. This friend is a good friend. He is a sailor, an American sailor, and he knows what goes on in ports. Roberto has a hunch.'

'What's a hunch?'

III

They landed from the *vapore* at the Porta St Elena, where the big ships lay, and cut through the public gardens. There seemed to be women on every seat, behind every tree; they had bright acquisitive eyes, and the air of marksmen alert for the moving targets, and men with an air of authority and swagger moved among them, keeping an eye on them like sergeants. Roberto quickened his pace.

The boy asked, 'Are they waiting to go on board?'

'They are waiting for friends,' Roberto said.

In a café near the Campo del Grappa a sailor sat over a glass of beer. He wore a double-breasted jacket and a peaked cap – he was an ordinary seaman, the boy could tell that, and he wondered whether he was a mate. The word 'mate' had always stuck in his head since the first sea story he had read.

'This is the young shoofa,'[5] Roberto said.

'I can't stay long.'

Roberto said to the boy, 'We have a small small business to discuss first. You just go off and get yourself a drink. And order a Strega for me.'

When the boy came back, the sailor was saying: 'Two thousand Camels,' and the boy momentarily had a vision of a vast desert, a little square of redcoats led by an officer with a lame leg, assaulted by savage tribesmen, and over the sand dunes the long line of the Camel Corps lurching to the rescue. He dug his own heels firmly into the flank of the leading camel (he was the only one who had known the route to lead them), and saw his father's face with sudden clarity looming ahead of him, a smear of mud like a two days' beard over the chin and cheeks. It was the face he had seen turning at the garden gate: it was a face that reminded him of he couldn't remember what.

'Same price. Same place,' Roberto said, and his father looked up at him with astonishment and joy, and his lips moved, but he was still too far away to hear the words.

'This jeezer,' Roberto said, 'is a Yank off the *U.S. Grant*.'

The boy turned his eyes unwillingly from the beleaguered square to the round pink shaven face under the peaked cap. 'He is the steward,' Roberto said, 'if you know what that means.'

'Any news of the kid's father?'

'Nothing.'

'You know I'm fond of kids,' the steward said, with an air of injured innocence, 'you know I'd help if I could, but I'm damned if I can see… I'm no flatfoot.'

'This is what I have been thinking,' Roberto said. 'His father arrived on Wednesday night. This is Saturday. If they have killed him – listen, kiddo, you mustn't mind me saying that: you and I know he is not dead, for why? Nobody bothers to hide a body. You remember that Englishman who was found shot in a gondola in the lagoon – he was not missing twelve hours. You do not have to hide bodies in Venice – you set them afloat.'

The boy listened without distress. The conversation had no reality – or rather it had the reality of a strip cartoon, of things that happened to other people.

'There's such a thing as lead,' the steward commented, glinting at the boy, and silence fell for a moment in their café, as though the argument itself had been tied carefully up and dropped over the side. The boy was back with the thousand camels charging down.

Roberto said: 'Well, we have to believe…'

'What can we do that the flatfoots can't?'

'If you wanted to hide a man in Venezia…'

'Why should you want to hide a man anywhere?'

'You're a fine jeezer,' Roberto said, 'but you have no imagination. If you had committed a murder and I knew about it, you might want to put me out of the way while you escaped.'

'I'd bump you off right away,' the steward said. 'I'd liquidate you.'

'Liquidate?' Roberto brooded. 'This boy's father was a policeman in Trieste. There is an awful lot of politics in Trieste.'

'It don't get us anywhere.'

Roberto took a look at the boy, but he was absorbed in something, leaning forward in his chair, bumping gently on his seat. Roberto said: 'If it is a body, it'll bob up somewhere. That is what the police hope. Fell into the canal. Death by natural causes. We just have to believe…'

'I'm ready to believe any damned thing you tell me if it'll help.'

'Venezia is easy to search when once you begin. You would not want to keep a live man in Venezia long. Why, that chap the Yugoslavs picked up in Rome. They didn't even keep him in Rome long. The police traced him as far as Padova.'

'You bet he is in Yugoslavia by now.'

'Then he had to go by boat, or by plane. What boats are in now, Hamstringer, or just gone?'

'There haven't been any out in the last three days, except your coasters. There's my ship – you don't suspect that, do you? There's an English ship from Malta. There's that new Italian ship on the Egyptian run – tourist. There's one of our War Transport ships (Marshall Aid). A French freighter. A Yugoslav…' He fell suddenly silent staring into his beer glass.

Just before he reached his father, a spear slid under his father's guard and he went down with the blade in his shoulder. Then the whole square broke into cheers, and the Mahdi's followers were scattered and fleeing over the plain, while he knelt by his father's body, looking down at the face… looking down at him thus, he would hardly have known him.

The steward said, 'I went on board there last night. They should have sailed twenty-four hours before.'

'Which?'

'The Yugoslav. The steward's a friend of mine. He said there'd been some trouble about stores.'

A Summary of Guy Elmes's Continuation

[*The following events are based on the action of the film, and so Roger Court's chief ally becomes a chambermaid called Roberta.*]

As the police continue to do little to try to find Major Court, Roberta's boyfriend, an anti-Communist American sailor named Joe Hamstringer, guesses that the most likely place to find him is in the Yugoslavian ship that has postponed its sailing, ostensibly because of trouble with cargo. Roberta urges him to revisit the ship and take a look around. At the same time, Roger daydreams about the pursuit of his father in the desert, a fantasy triggered by Roger's misunderstanding about the Camels (a brand of American cigarettes) which Hamstringer has sold to the steward of the Yugoslavian freighter on his last visit to the ship. Roger dreams about riding a camel across the desert sands to rescue him after Major Court has been wounded by an Arab's spear. But in Roger's fantasy, inspired by the comic papers, once he reaches his father, he fails to recognise his face, because it is dirty and unshaven. At this point he realises that the sick man he told the police was not his father was unrecognisable only because of his two days' growth of beard. The realisation that he may have actually seen his father the day before in the seedy apartment room in the Rialto district induces a kind of fever in Roger, and Roberta and Hamstringer decide to take him home after Roger insists that the man he has seen was in fact his father. But Roberta ignores Roger, as she tries to catch up with Hamstringer, who is angry that, because of the boy's presence, he and Roberta have not made love as they usually do on her day off. Attempting to placate her boyfriend, she loses sight of Roger, who hangs back on the busy street and gets separated from the couple. He then decides to walk back on his own to his temporary home at the British consulate. Near the Doge's Palace, Roger lingers to watch a lurid puppet show depicting two knights in mortal combat, and he is retrieved there by Roberta and Hamstringer.

Safely back at the home of the British Consul, Roger is angered by the Consul's questions as to his recent whereabouts, observing that this father has the same weasel eyes as his son, Morgan. Roger offers a surly response that he has been out for a walk, a reply which prompts the Consul to suggest that he may not let Roger go out again without permission. Later that night, unable to sleep, Roger sneaks out of the bedroom he is sharing with Morgan, determined to return to the apartment across the Rialto bridge where, he is now convinced, he has recently seen his father, sick and unshaven. He is bent on proving to the incredulous couple that he really has seen his father there, despite their scepticism. But in Roger's mind, his father is the captive of the comic paper villain, Mr Hogan, whom Roger now confuses with the doctor who, during their first meeting, kindly bought him an ice cream and fashioned a ring of string for both their fingers, as a symbol of friendship. But after Roger's second meeting, when the doctor was questioned by the police while he was supposedly treating the two sick patients in the apartment near the Rialto, the doctor's darker side begins to impose itself upon Roger's consciousness.

Roger manages to calm his own fears as he walks through Venice later that night, soon arriving at the block he is looking for, quickly finding the stairs leading to the top-floor apartment where his father was. Choosing the middle of three entrance doors, Roger arrives in the correct apartment, and finds it now nearly empty, with no sign that his father has been sleeping there. All the other rooms in the apartment are in darkness, but Roger is too short to reach the light-switch. Yet he feels compelled to find his father before Mr Hogan does.

Desperately calling, 'Papa,' his voice echoes in the naked apartment, and Roger realises that he is too late – the doctor and his father are not there, and, weeping, he collapses to the floor. A short time passes before Joe Hamstringer calls out from the threshold, 'Major Court,' soon coming across Roger's trembling body. After a nocturnal walk with Hamstringer through the deserted streets and docks, Roger notices that it is now three in the morning. When Roger wakes up, he finds himself in Roberta's apartment, where he sees Hamstringer sitting at a table, fabricating an incendiary bomb.

The scene shifts to a cabin of the Yugoslavian ship which Hamstringer and Roger have passed earlier that morning on their way to Roberta's apartment. Major Court, awake and relatively clear-headed, is unsure how much time has elapsed since he was drugged. He notices that the doctor is not in the cabin, but he sees Peskovitch, finally awake and calling for a glass of water, which, because the guard has fallen asleep, Court gets for him. The latter gives a sign that he will pretend to be asleep, so Court realises that the old Balkan conspirator is going to keep on fighting. He also realizes that his sight of Roger was not a dream.

At daybreak, the doctor returns, looking sicker than ever, telling Court that soon he will have to do without his medical care. He tells Court that after the police visit and the fuss about the child, the Yugoslavian captors have decided to sail at noon for Yugoslavia with Court and Peskovitch. The doctor brings milk and sandwiches for the two prisoners, but Peskovitch pretends to be unconscious. The guard, now awake, greedily eats Peskovitch's meal. With the growing light, Court looks out of the porthole and notices a man rowing a one-person *sandola*. It is Hamstringer, getting ready to board the ship.

Later, at the main police bureau, the Chief of Police, a fat Sicilian, is very pleased to see Roger, accompanied by Roberta, since with Roger's return it will now be possible to avert an embarrassing story in the Venice newspapers. The Chief telephones the Consul-General with the news that Roger has been brought in to the station by Roberta, who identifies herself as a Yugoslavian refugee, showing her identity card.

The Commissioner soon agrees with Roberta that Major Court and Peskovitch must be prisoners on the Yugoslavian ship, although he believes it impossible to interfere with the ship's scheduled departure at noon, since it would be illegal to board what is, in effect, Yugoslavian territory, adding that the only way they could legally board the ship would be if a fire broke out on board.

The next scene opens at ten-forty in the morning, as Hamstringer offers the steward a good deal in blackmarket nylon stockings. The ship is at anchor near the island of San Giorgio, and Hamstringer observes a group of tourists through the porthole, as he gets ready to set off the incendiary bomb to stop the ship from sailing at noon. At a quarter to twelve, a Yugoslavian civilian, wearing a raincoat and fedora, enters the steward's cabin, notices the nylons, utters a few Slavic words to the steward, then leaves the cabin. The second mate scolds the steward for disobeying the order to let no outsiders on board. The steward returns with the news that Hamstringer will have to be brought back to port with the pilot after their departure. Feigning a need for fresh air, Hamstringer steps briefly outside the cabin and tosses the incendiary bomb into the storeroom, and as he returns to the cabin, he fells the steward with a punch to the jaw.

At twelve-fifteen, the Commissioner suggests that since nothing can be done about the ship, Roger should be returned to the British consulate. News comes that the Yugoslavs have put out the fire and that the fireboats will not be permitted to move, since no sirens have sounded. Roberta observes Roger sitting in the prow of one of the fireboats and wonders how to break the news to him that they can do nothing. She also wonders how she can try to prevent Roger's disappointment and ultimate disillusionment with the adult world to which she belongs. Yet, ironically, all the while that Roberta is fretting about having to reveal to Roger the unromantic, unheroic nature of the adult world, Roger looks admiringly at Roberta, thinking of her as Joe Hamstringer's girl. A hero's girl. When Roger asks whether it is true the fireboats can reach over seventy miles an hour, she humours him, troubled that she will soon have to tell him that they will not be setting out after Mr Hogan; that he will soon have to get down from the speedboat that the Commissioner has asked him to sit in so as to be the first to enter the ship and identify his father. Then suddenly the sirens sound, set off by Hamstringer before he leapt into the water, and the fireboats now go into action.

Hearing the sirens, Major Court asks the doctor what is happening. The guard has left the cabin to find out, and from the porthole the doctor observes Hamstringer swimming towards the police speedboat and being helped aboard. The gloomy doctor, against his will, is forced to admit, given Hamstringer's heroic actions, that the inevitable can be post-poned or even conquered, but he will do nothing to save himself. He decides not to resist, but instead, to sink, like Venice, like all the rest of the world. At that moment he sees an armada of fireboats appearing from under the Accademia bridge, 'passing the *Santa Maria della Salute*, advancing in the dazzling glare of noon. The sun, unexpectedly, had triumphed over the clouds... the boats advanced with their warlike prows raised above the foaming water, like a row of chanticleers about to fling themselves upon their opponents'. Here Elmes's diction rises to true Cold-War melodramatic heights, as the doctor tells Major Court that luck is on his side. Catching sight of Roger in the boat, the doctor observes to himself that this will be their third meeting. He contrasts his own despairing eyes with the trusting, hopeful eyes of Roger and, awakened from his death-wish reverie by the click of the cocked gun, he turns and flings himself upon the guard, taking a bullet to the heart, while as Peskovitch knocks the gun to the ground, the police, with Roger in tow, fling open the cabin door.

Major Court solemnly shakes hands with his son, but no one notices the doctor, lying dead, his hand extended in an indeterminate gesture of either affirmation or denial, with a string tied around one of his fingers. Around Roger's finger, worn like a ring, is the other half of that piece of string, which the doctor gave him.

Notes

No Man's Land

1. A skiing town in the Harz Mountains.

2. Navy, Army and Air Force Institutes. Shops and recreational establishments for service personnel established in 1921 by the British Government.

3. After the Second World War, Germany was divided into three separate occupation zones: British, American and Russian. French zones were later carved out of the British and American zones.

4. Winston Churchill's most famous, if not his first, reference to the 'Iron Curtain' occurred during a speech delivered at Westminster College, Fulton, Missouri, on 5th March 1946.

5. Greene visited many shrines that commemorated visions of Mary, but the original of the Ilsenhof shrine would appear to be the shrine at Tre Fontane, a grotto on a hillside near Rome. Greene says he visited the shrine, and refers to Mary's appearing to three children there in 1947.

6. Compare Matthew 17: 22: 'The Son of Man shall be betrayed into the hands of men.'

7. Royal Army Service Corps.

8. Evidently Greene had not entirely forgiven John Boynton Priestley (1894–1984) for objecting to his caricature figure, Quin Savory, in *Stamboul Train* (1932). Greene's friend Evelyn Waugh refers to Priestley as one who sees himself 'as the epitome of the Common Man'.

9. British Armed Forces money, not legal tender outside the NAAFI.

10. See *Odes*, I: 5.

11. Heinemann was Greene's publisher, and the set of Turgenev that Greene owned and annotated, in Constance Garnett's translation, was also published by Heinemann.

12. The MKVD was the National Commissariat for Internal Affairs, i.e. the Soviet secret police that later became the KGB.

13. From *A Lear of the Steppes*, Chapter 18.

14. From the opening letter of Turgenev's story 'Faust'.

The Stranger's Hand

1. The villain in the children's adventure tale Roger has been reading.

2. Motor-racing circuit in Weybridge, Surrey, which opened in 1907 and closed at the outbreak of the Second World War in 1939.

3. 'Leg Before Wicket': an umpire's decision that the ball would have hit the wicket had it not been impeded by the batsman's leg.

4. Oswald Spengler's (1880–1936) influential work, published in an English translation in 1926–28, theorised the inevitable decline of Western civilisation.

5. Another example of Roberto's penchant for 'extraordinary words', possibly derived from the Italian *ciuffo*, 'a wisp of hair'.

Biographical note

Henry Graham Greene was born in Berkhamsted, Hertford-shire, in 1904 to Charles Greene, headmaster of Berkhamsted School, and Marion Raymond, cousin of the author Robert Louis Stevenson. Greene was educated at his father's school before going up to Oxford, where he studied Modern History at Balliol College. During his time there he published *Babbling April* (1925), a book of verse, as well as numerous articles in a student magazine.

In 1926 Greene converted to Catholicism, and his fascination with the faith was to influence many of his future works. Around the same time, he moved to London and took up a position with *The Times*, where he remained until 1930. He then devoted himself to writing, but it was not until his fourth novel, *Stamboul Train* (1932), that he received critical acclaim. By the time of his appointment as literary editor of the *Spectator* in 1940, he was recognised as a writer of considerable talent and versatility, having already published *England Made Me* (1935), *Journey Without Maps* (1936), which details his travels through Liberia, *Brighton Rock* (1938) and *The Confidential Agent* (1939). One of his most famous novels, *The Power and the Glory*, appeared in 1940; his fictional treatment of religious persecution in Mexico caused it to be condemned by the Vatican.

During the Second World War Greene worked for the Foreign Office, and was stationed in Sierra Leone from 1941 to 1943. His experiences there led him to write *The Heart of the Matter* (1948), which he set in West Africa. He followed this with, among others, *The End of the Affair* (1951), *The Quiet American* (1955) and *Our Man in Havana* (1958). He also wrote a number of travel pieces, short stories, articles, plays and film treatments, including *The Third Man* (1950), which he reworked into a novel, and *No Man's Land* (1950).

Greene was awarded the Order of Merit and made a Companion of Honour for his services to literature. He died in April 1991.

Dr James Sexton is a lecturer at Camosun College, Victoria, British Columbia and, since 2002, a visiting *Maître de conférences* at l'Université du Sud, Toulon-Var, during the winter term. He is a specialist in Renaissance, Modern and Utopian literature, and has published a number of articles and scholarly editions, mostly on Aldous Huxley.

HESPERUS PRESS

Hesperus Press, as suggested by the Latin motto, is committed to bringing near what is far – far both in space and time. Works written by the greatest authors, and unjustly neglected or simply little known in the English-speaking world, are made accessible through new translations and a completely fresh editorial approach. Through these classic works, the reader is introduced to the greatest writers from all times and all cultures.

For more information on Hesperus Press, please visit our website:
www.hesperuspress.com

ET REMOTISSIMA PROPE

MODERN VOICES